DEFENDED BY A DUKE

The Beresford Adventures
Book 6

Cheryl Bolen

Text by Cheryl Bolen
Cover by Dar Albert

Dragonblade Publishing, Inc. is an imprint of Kathryn Le Veque Novels, Inc.
P.O. Box 23
Moreno Valley, CA 92556
ceo@dragonbladepublishing.com

Produced in the United States of America

First Edition September 2023
Trade Paperback Edition

ARE YOU SIGNED UP FOR DRAGONBLADE'S BLOG?

You'll get the latest news and information on exclusive giveaways, exclusive excerpts, coming releases, sales, free books, cover reveals and more.

Check out our complete list of authors, too!

No spam, no junk. That's a promise!

Sign Up Here

www.dragonbladepublishing.com

Dearest Reader;

Thank you for your support of a small press. At Dragonblade Publishing, we strive to bring you the highest quality Historical Romance from some of the best authors in the business. Without your support, there is no 'us', so we sincerely hope you adore these stories and find some new favorite authors along the way.

Happy Reading!

CEO, Dragonblade Publishing

Additional Dragonblade books by Author Cheryl Bolen

The Beresford Adventures

Lady Mary's Dangerous Encounter (Book 1)
My Lord Protector (Book 2)
With a Little Help from My Lord (Book 3)
Rescued by a Rake (Book 4)
Vindicated by a Viscount (Book 5)
Defended by a Duke (Book 6)

CHAPTER ONE

RICHARD HARWOOD, THE 6th Duke of Bentley, had just descended the curving staircase at his palatial Grosvenor Square townhouse and was expected for a noon meeting at the Mayfair home of his House of Lords colleague, the Earl of Devere, when he saw the morning's post had come. He was all but certain of the content of the correspondence. Since it was the Season, there would be no fewer than half a dozen invitations to balls.

It grew tedious being the most sought-after bachelor in London. Every matchmaking mother in the Capital wished to align her daughter with the Duke of Bentley. And Bentley was well aware his wealth and title accounted for his desirability—not necessarily the man himself.

He quickly scanned the stack. Balls all. He had no wish to attend any of them. In fact, the thing he enjoyed least was attending balls. Equally as loathsome was being forced to converse—if one could call it that—with empty-headed debutantes.

Though most of his friends had now married, Bentley was coming to believe he was too entrenched in his bachelorhood to ever wed. What was the likelihood of a woman snaring his heart when such an occurrence had failed to happen in his thirty years? Not once had he found a woman with whom he could imagine spending the rest of his life. And God only knew how many dozens had tried since he inherited the title ten years earlier.

He slung the invitations back down on the sideboard, slipped on his gloves, took the proffered hat and coat procured by the footman, and left his house. He'd chosen the coach today because of the mists and threat of rain.

Ten minutes later, he'd reached Devere House. He was ten minutes early. Bentley prided himself on his punctuality. "My Lord Devere will meet you and Lord Rockingham in the library presently," the butler told him. "Lord Rockingham's not here yet."

While showing Bentley to the library, the butler led him past a salon where a group of women gathered. Devere's wife was that rare creature: a woman who revered politics and was knowledgeable about the workings of government. A pity Devere had snagged the beauty first. Now, that was a woman who could have stolen Bentley's affections with no effort whatsoever.

As he passed the chamber, he heard a melodious voice saying something that caused him to stop in his stride. The voice did *not* belong to Lady Caroline Devere.

"The right to learn to read and write should no more be limited than the right to breathe. All the ills in our society could be eliminated if we made education available universally. Only in an educated citizenry can depravities be eradicated."

Curious to see who was speaking, he retraced his steps and peered into the chamber. A young woman, hardly more than a girl, was the speaker. At first he could not believe such wisdom could come from a female of such youth.

He continued watching as she spoke. The young woman was stunning.

There was nothing flashy or exotic about her. In many ways, she was a quintessential English young lady. If taken individually, her features were average. Medium brown hair. Medium height. Medium body structure. Eyes a common green. Yet, when feathered together, those features created something quite out of the ordinary.

Her flawless face was nothing short of perfection. Her lips might be a trifle too thin, but when she smiled at Lady Devere, deep dimples and the most beautiful teeth he'd ever seen were revealed. It was a smile that could light up an entire room.

He found himself smiling and nodding as she continued. Never mind that she was beginning to attack those, like him, who held rank.

"Those of us who hail from aristocratic families," she continued, "have an obligation to see to it that those who toil in our homes and on our lands have the opportunity to become educated. I believe, as I know those of you in this chamber today do, Parliament must move to grant these rights to all British citizens—not simply grant, but mandate and fund the means of obtaining this basic right." The young beauty then gracefully moved to her seat.

Like one transfixed by a phenomenon, he was compelled to look at her. Until Devere sidled up to him. "Early as usual, Bentley."

Bentley extracted his watch and eyed it. "As it happens, my good man, it's twelve o'clock straight up."

As they walked toward the Devere library, Lord Rockingham came. Then the three men entered the library, and Devere closed the door behind them. They had gathered to discuss the points in a speech that Rockingham was to deliver in the House of Lords later in the day, but Bentley's thoughts were dominated by one intelligent and beautiful young woman.

"Your countess has started a bluestocking group here at Devere House?" Bentley asked his host.

Devere chuckled. "Pray, don't say that in front of Caro. She doesn't fancy herself a bluestocking; she's a political devotee. Her late father, you may recall, was rather important in the House of Commons a few years back."

Bentley nodded. "Oh, yes. Before the tragic fire." He cleared his throat. "Who was the young lady promulgating universal education?"

"That would be my youngest Beresford cousin, Emily," Devere said. "She came to town to be presented to the queen, which she's done. I believe the plan—at least by her brother, who's her guardian—was for her to capture a husband this Season. The lady, lamentably, is not obliging. She *is* a bit of a bluestocking and has not enjoyed the balls and attending Almack's, though I'm told she has been a great success with the young men who've danced attendance upon her. I'm happy she's not staying with us. The place would be swarming with young men bearing nosegays and poorly written poetry."

Bentley tried to sound casual. "Where is she staying?"

Devere's solemn gaze flicked to him. "Back and forth between her sisters, Lady Lucy Montague and Lady Georgiana Churston."

"Is that the one who recently married Lord Churston?" Bentley asked.

"Yes."

"How is it that all acquisitions to the Beresford family manage to be Whigs?" Bentley asked. "Do you forbid Tories to call upon your females?"

"I dare say we've just been lucky." Devere eyed the other man. "Imagine my joy when I learned that Rockingham meant to marry my youngest sister."

"It also helped that I was your closest friend," Lord Rockingham said.

"Speaking of friends, why did you find it necessary last night to go to White's?" Rockingham asked. "I thought your friends only went to Brooks's."

Devere did not answer for a moment. It was as if he were trying to weigh his words carefully before he spoke. "It's too early for me to speak, but I suspect the Tories are up to something that could harm the kingdom."

"You know you can count on my assistance in anything," Rockingham said.

"And on mine," Bentley added. He had to own, his curiosity had been nudged.

"Now," Devere said, eyeing Rockingham, "about that speech you're scheduled to give this afternoon . . ."

"Because you two are among the most well-respected Whigs in the House of Lords, I want to make sure we're on the same page before I shake things up rather dramatically," Rockingham said.

Dramatically? Now Rockingham had Bentley's full attention. "Go on."

"Though I have an inkling of what you're going to address, I expect it's the details we need to agree upon," Devere said.

"It wasn't easy to obtain, but I've gathered some frightfully alarming figures on the number of children who have died laboring in factories." Rockingham's voice strengthened with resolve. "We must establish regulations that address this."

"It's a pity we can't abolish it altogether," Bentley said.

"I agree," Devere added.

"You two are too idealistic. But while I, too, wish for abolishment, I'm more pragmatic than you," Rockingham said.

Devere nodded. "That's why you're so effective a leader of the Whigs. You've mastered the art of compromise."

"The day can't come too soon when we can eradicate children from the work force." Bentley thought of the word *eradicate.* Minutes ago the Stunner had used it when speaking of universal education. *An educated citizenry would eradicate depravities.* It seemed as if he and the beauty were possessed of like minds.

It was a rarity to find a woman who thought of anything but frocks. It was even more of a rarity to find a woman whose views so closely mirrored his own.

"Of course we are in complete agreement with you, Bentley," Rockingham said. "But we must win our reforms in increments."

Devere indicated his agreement. "I still recall Lord Whittington's response when we brought up the subject of children dying in factories."

Bentley winced. "Oh, yes. Horrifying. *They're just little orphans no one cares about.* Would that we could eradicate the ills that contribute to the proliferation of orphans."

"If only we could," Devere lamented.

"We're on the right road," Rockingham said. "I believe one day that can happen. We're taking the first steps now."

"So, Rockingham, what are you going to touch on in today's speech? Will you refer to the alarming number of child deaths in those factories?" Devere asked.

"I must."

The two other men nodded in agreement.

"Then what kind of limits will you propose?" Bentley asked.

Rockingham held out an index finger and began to enumerate his points. "First, I propose establishing an entry age of . . . what do you gentlemen think is reasonable?"

"Anything under the age of twelve is not acceptable to me," Bentley said.

Devere nodded. "I agree."

"Then my proposal will be limiting the age to twelve and above."

"What else?" Bentley asked.

"I would ask that those children be paid at least three-quarters of what an adult earns."

The two others indicated their agreement.

"Will you recommend a punitive clause?"

"I must. What would you suggest?"

"First, fines."

"And to be effective, they need to be significant," Devere said.

Rockingham eyed his friend. "How significant?"

"I'd say start with the equivalent of an adult's annual salary."

"I don't think that's punitive enough," Bentley said.

Rockingham nodded. "I agree. Those men earn less in a year than the average peer wagers in one hour at Faro. Their wages are pitiably insignificant—as little as five-and-twenty pounds a year."

Bentley groaned. "My youngest stable hands earn more than that."

"Ah, but you, my friend, are enlightened," Devere said. "Sadly, we cannot say the same about most members of the House of Lords. That's why we Whigs are in the minority."

"Unfortunately, the lords are rather a self-serving lot," Rockingham added. "I know of no other members, other than our illustrious Duke of Bentley, who furnishes such luxurious living accommodations for his grooms."

"Not just grooms," Bentley said. "All of my servants enjoy generous salaries and comfortable living quarters."

"I know you want to set an admirable example, but many peers will say it's easy for you to do so because your wealth is so vast."

Bentley shrugged. "That's fair enough."

"The same could be said for Devere," Rockingham pointed out. "He's generous to his servants, and he happens to be exceedingly rich."

"Back to the matter of penalties . . ." Devere said. "What if it's not monetary?"

Bentley's brows lowered. "Care to elaborate?"

"What if non-compliance results in a shutdown of the factory?"

"I like it," Bentley said, "But that will never pass."

Rockingham's lips folded. "You're probably right."

An amused look swiped across Devere's face. "Ah, but that's where the art of compromise comes in. Threaten first with shutdowns, and later settle for a significant fine."

"Brilliant," Bentley said. "How significant?"

"At least a hundred guineas per infraction," Rockingham answered.

"Then we start off by threatening shutdowns but settle for a hundred quid?" Devere asked.

His friend nodded.

They continued ironing out the details of Rockingham's plan, but Bentley's thoughts kept straying to the Stunner. Miss Emily Beresford. He had to meet her, to speak to her, to find out if she really was as perfect as he first suspected.

After they satisfied themselves on Rockingham's speech and were leaving Devere's library, he approached Devere. "Would you do me the goodness of making introductions between me and Miss Emily Beresford?"

Devere gave him a quizzing look, then gathered his composure. "Of course, Your Grace."

When they reached the salon, the half a dozen ladies gathered there were standing and appeared to be saying farewells. The former Harriett Beresford, now Lady Rockingham, greeted Bentley before linking her arm to her husband's and taking her leave. The former Lucy Beresford, now Lady Montague, and her sister, Georgiana, now Lady Churston, stood talking to their hostess, Lady Devere, along with the lovely Emily Beresford, whom Lord Devere addressed. "Emily, may we borrow you for a moment?"

She turned to her cousin and bestowed one of her radiant smiles upon him. "Of course, my lord." She strolled up to the pair of them. Though she was slenderer than Bentley typically preferred a woman to be, her elegance of dress and of bearing more than compensated for her lack of curvature.

Devere eyed Bentley. "Your Grace, it is my honor to present to you my cousin, Miss Emily Beresford." Turning to the beautiful young woman, Devere said, "my friend and colleague, the Duke of Bentley."

Her large lichen eyes flashed with what could only be recognition of his name—a disappointment to him. Was she to be just another maiden marking him as a matrimonial catch?

"It's an honor to make your acquaintance, Your Grace. I've been anxious to meet you." She turned to Devere, who was titular head of the Beresford family. "Why did you not tell me you were acquainted with the duke?"

"I knew not that you had any interest in meeting him. You

haven't shown the slightest regard for any of the bachelors I've introduced you to."

She gave a mock frown. "Not for matrimonial purposes. Surely you know me better than that. I wish to commend him."

"Commend him?" Devere asked.

The two were carrying on this conversation as if Bentley weren't present.

"Yes." She then turned to Bentley. "I've been a great admirer of you, Your Grace."

As popular as Bentley was with debutants, none had ever come out with such a declaration on their first meeting. Miss Emily Beresford must be an exceptionally brazen young woman.

"Pray, Miss Beresford, why do you say that?" It suddenly occurred to him that she, like Devere's wife, might be interested in Parliament. Perhaps she admired his legislative agenda.

"Your generosity to your servants is legendary. I should like to find out all the details about it."

This lady was, indeed, a singular young woman. No maiden he'd ever encountered was possessed of this kind of inquiring mind. "Perhaps we could do so during a drive in the park."

"I should adore that."

As would he. He almost asked if he could collect her that very afternoon, but he needed to support Rockingham in the House of Lords this afternoon. "Are you free tomorrow afternoon?"

"I am."

"Where can I collect you?"

"I'm at Montague House."

"Then it will be my honor to see you there tomorrow afternoon."

His step was lighter than normal when he left Devere House a few minutes later. He felt like a schoolboy giddy with anticipation. That's the effect Miss Emily Beresford had upon him. How in the devil was it that a daytime visit to pay a call in some stuffy parlor filled him with more excitement than his horse winning the derby?

CHAPTER TWO

IN THESE THREE weeks she'd spent in the Capital, prospective husbands had been shoved her way every day and every night. Not one of the young men had ever appealed to Miss Emily Beresford on any level.

Until she met the Duke of Bentley.

She was well aware others would say his lofty rank and vast wealth accounted for her deep attraction to him. But, quite honestly, many of the men who'd made romantic overtures toward her were possessed of rank and wealth. The Duke of Bentley stood out from the others because his empathy for the less fortunate seemed to exactly match her own. She had decided it would be her life's mission to do what she could to alleviate misfortune and ignorance. From what she'd heard of the duke, he shared her vision to help mankind.

She had long wanted to meet him and pick his brain, but now that she'd met him, the attraction went much deeper than shared interests. The man possessed great physical appeal. For some reason, she'd expected him to be quite old, not a fine-looking man of no more than thirty years.

Despite his clothing of impeccable good taste, there was something rugged about him. She could almost picture him at the bow of a privateer's ship, cutlass in hand. Perhaps it was his coloring that contributed to his utter masculinity. His black hair was matched by eyes of the same color. And though he had no doubt shaved that morning, a dark shadow of stubble stained his fair face.

Even his build bespoke masculinity. He was as tall as Devere, who was above average in height, but he seemed shorter because of his musculature. His shoulders formed a broad T crowning a body of rock-solid arms and legs as substantial as marble pillars. Yet, surprisingly, all those muscles tapered to a lean waist.

Because the Duke of Bentley was going to call upon her, it was imperative that she look her best. "Please, Maggie," she said to her maid, "you must render me pretty today." Emily was not given to long primping sessions of dressing her hair, pinching her cheeks, and dousing herself with French perfumes. Not until today.

Maggie emitted a long guffaw. "I never seen you when you weren't the prettiest girl in the kingdom—save for Georgiana, who looks almost just like you. Methinks you must have met The One. Is he to call on you today?"

Emily's heart fluttered at the mention of The One. She hadn't put it to words, but she thought the Duke of Bentley might, indeed, be The One. He could quite possibly be the man with whom she would like to spend the rest of her life.

The very notion sent her pulse galloping. She would not come out and admit the duke was The One. But neither could she say he wasn't. To herself, she could admit he was the most desirable man she'd ever encountered. "I'm to ride in the park with him today."

"Then you must wear the pelisse you say is asparagus colored. It do be chilly, and that color brings out yer eyes, not that a pretty thing like you needs any help. You could wear a potato sack and be beautiful."

"I'm blessed to have you, dearest Maggie."

After her maid had styled her hair most attractively and assisted her in dressing, Emily said, "I'd like Mama's scent today." She wished to smell of spring roses. After all, the man who could possibly be her future husband was to sit quite close to her in the carriage. This was the first time in her life she'd anxiously anticipated being physically close to a man.

When the duke was announced, her heartbeat accelerated. She took one last glance into her looking glass. Though she knew her appearance could not be improved upon, she wished there was something about her that would demand a man take notice. Her looks were, to her, nothing out of the ordinary. In fact, she'd become accustomed to hearing herself described as wholesome-looking.

She'd always been astonished that men seemed to prefer her above most others—not that she'd ever been interested in any of those who wished to court her. Before. Before she met the Duke of Bentley. She most sincerely hoped His Grace would favor her in exactly the same way she favored him.

Her inner trembling extended even to her hand gripping the banister as she descended the stairway. With each downward step, she came closer to the duke, who stood in the foyer gazing up at her, a soft smile on his face.

"Good day to you, Miss Beresford," he said. "How I wish the day were as lovely as you, but, alas, it's gray and cold."

Flirting, to Emily, was as alien as the Russian language, but today she would flirt. "I declare that any day spent with Your Grace will be free from dreariness. I have been looking forward to it."

He could not have looked more pleased had she given him the Crown Jewels. It was then that she noticed he held a nosegay of early spring blooms. "For you, Miss Beresford."

"How thoughtful of you. They're lovely. I'll just have the footman put them in water while we're gone."

"I came in the barouche today," he said, "so I could be free to give you my undivided attention."

Exactly what she had hoped for. His coachman, instead of him, would deal with snarled traffic at the park's entrance while he and she furthered their acquaintance.

Though they had escaped rain, blustery, cool winds rendered it a fairly unpleasant day, but she would not let trifles like that detract from her enjoyment of having the Duke of Bentley all to herself. Even so, she was thankful she'd brought the ermine muff to keep her hands warm.

He offered his hand to climb into the conveyance, and when she set her hand in his, warmth and something indefinably lovely spread within her.

"I hope you don't mind if I sit next to you," he said, "but I thought it would help block some of the cold."

She smiled into his dark eyes. "That should make the elements much more tolerable." Truth be told, this would be the first time for her to be so close to a man. In the past, such a prospect would never have been welcomed; with the Duke of Bentley, it was most heartily embraced.

He came to sit next to her and nodded at his driver to begin. "Now, my dear Miss Beresford, what is it you wished to ask me?"

"I've been told that all of your servants at Warfield Abbey are paid at least twice that of what servants in comparable estates receive, and they are also given two days off each week. Can all of this be true?"

"It is true, but I see nothing significant about it. It's the least men of wealth can do for those who toil for us."

"It just occurred to me—don't most dukes own several properties?"

"I suppose so."

"What other properties do you oversee besides Warfield?"

He did not respond for a moment. "There's the castle in Ireland, the villa at Twickenham on the Thames, the Grosvenor Square house, a hunting lodge in Scotland, and two or three manor houses scattered about England that were inherited from various branches of the Harwood family."

Just as she suspected. "And are all of your servants in all those residences compensated as well as the ones at Warfield?"

"Of course."

"I commend you on the example you're setting. I don't look upon it as a religious action as much as a humanitarian one, but I am always reminded of Matthew's verse: *Inasmuch as ye have done it unto one of the least of these my brethren, ye have done it unto me."* She paused to shake her head. "I wonder what it would take for other noblemen to follow your lead?"

"I've heard that your brother has. Were you an influence in that decision-making process?"

It was a moment before she answered. "I may have made the initial suggestion, but my brother is kind, and he is progressive. Any generosity he's initiated is his own doing."

"I've also heard about his impressive agricultural improvements."

"He's terribly resourceful. I do lament that he won't stand for the House of Commons. There's no limit to all the good he could accomplish."

"We could certainly use more Whigs." He met her gaze. "I do detect your interest in reforms."

Her cheeks heated. "You overheard my vituperative comments yesterday morning about education for all?"

"I was impressed. You expressed ideas I wish I had expressed and with far more eloquence. Would that women like you could serve in Parliament."

"I could never stand up in Parliament to express my opinions. It's vastly different doing so among my family members and a few other like-minded women."

"Then, too, words have no cost; actions are far more dear—not that I'm discrediting you in any way."

"Oh, but you're right, Your Grace. It's easy to spout out platitudes. I assure you I'm committed to the things I promulgate. I spend much of my pin money establishing and maintaining a small school for young ladies back in Lincolnshire. I'm proud to say my brother has started schools for lads at each of the properties belonging to our branch of the Beresford Family."

"A not insignificant endeavor. I know the Beresfords own

thousands of acres throughout England."

"Would that there were more men like you and my brother." She frowned. "I do wish James would serve in Parliament."

They had reached Hyde Park, and in spite of the gray skies, cool temperatures, and unpleasantly strong winds, a number of phaetons, curricles, and saddle horses clogged the entrance. Men held onto their hats, and many of the young ladies had lifted hoods to their cloaks to warm their chilled ears.

He chuckled. "You are certainly passionate about reforms. Most women do not share your interest."

She whipped around to face him. "Sadly, that can also be said about most men. You are rather singular, Your Grace."

"But it's my most fervent hope not to be singular."

"Yes, I understand. If only more men were in agreement with you. Do you think the day will ever come?"

Those impressive shoulders of his shrugged. "I do think reform is inevitable. After all, we aristocrats are seriously outnumbered. The masses will one day demand basic rights. On the other hand, it's human nature to be greedy. Man will always seek self-interests."

He referred to aristocrats. Sometimes she was ashamed to hail from an aristocratic family—even though hers was known for its benevolence. "But, in that, Your Grace, I sense you are not like other men."

"Oh, but I am greedy."

She looked up into his profile, admiring his aquiline nose. "About what?'

"About beautiful women from Lincolnshire. You see, I choose not to share you."

His words, coming so early in their acquaintance, stunned her. Could he, indeed, feel possessive toward her? The very notion made her feel like a fairy princess. Even more stunning was his sentiment—for she felt the very same about him. This intimacy with the Duke of Bentley made her deliriously happy.

What began with admiration of his actions had somehow

quickly transferred to physical desire. Everything about this man appealed to her. The simple touch of her legs alongside his affected her profoundly. The tenor of his manly voice awakened her to his undeniable virility. And when those black eyes of his peered into hers, an earthquake of emotions rumbled her insides.

She was bereft of a response. Her first instinct had been to admit she also cherished this time alone with him, which was strange, considering never before had she wanted to be alone with any man.

She possessed enough sense to know she must cling to her pride. It wouldn't do to allow the duke to know how foolishly she was attracted to him. After all, she'd only met him the previous day. She knew enough of the *ton* to know a man in his position would be the biggest matrimonial prize in the kingdom. He would certainly be no stranger to women's abundant flirtations.

As difficult as it would be, she must stand apart from those women who, no doubt, freely offered themselves to him.

"I believe the Duke of Bentley is quite the flatterer."

"Normally, I'm not."

Her heartbeat quickened. Was it possible he was as affected by her as she was by him? Or was he simply accustomed to such flirtations? She was much too much the novice at these affairs to know.

She longed to tell him she relished being alone with him, that she, too, wished to be greedy about her time with him, but she must be mindful of just how much he was used to being the object of women's desires.

At the same time, she must not alienate him. He must understand his companionship was most agreeable to her. "Then, Your Grace, I admit I'm flattered by your attentions."

From time to time, the duke would acknowledge passersby with a simple nod but would not disturb his conversation with her by stopping to exchange pleasantries with any of the others.

When a lull in their conversation occurred, she did not hesitate to keep it going. "I read in this morning's *Chronicle* about

Lord Rockingham's speech in the House of Lords yesterday," she said. "Is that what you gentlemen were discussing with my cousin when we met?"

"It was."

"I have never been more moved or in more agreement with anything than I was by that overwhelmingly brilliant speech. What was the reception to it?"

His shoulders slumped. "Not what we had hoped. It seems not only are the Whigs in the minority, but so are our progressive ideas."

"The welfare of children should not be a progressive idea but a birthright."

"Yes. I know. It's as you said yesterday: *Only in an educated citizenry can depravities be eradicated.*"

He'd remembered her exact words! That most definitely decided it. This man was without any doubt The One. It was as if identical scripts ran through each of their brains. What was the likelihood any other man in the kingdom thought like she did? In addition to that commonality, she'd never met a man with greater physical appeal.

She could no longer be a coy debutante. "Oh, Bentley, you're a man after my own heart!" She hadn't meant to address him by the name Devere used. It seemed too intimate in view of their brief acquaintance. Blood rushed to her cheeks. She'd been far too forward.

"I like it when you address me more informally," he said in a husky murmur. His black eyes held her as if by chains. She could not have looked away were the carriage in flames. Then he did something which caused her heartbeat to stampede. His gaze never leaving hers, his hand caressed her cheek.

Then she did something so unexpected she mortified herself. When his hand moved away, she took it and pressed her lips to it.

A slow, provocative smile spread on his handsome face. "Miss Emily Beresford pleases me very much."

WAS IT ONLY the previous day he was lamenting that he would never marry? How could it be that in thirty years he'd never once met a woman who could claim his heart, and now in a single day he'd come to crave one very young and exceedingly appealing young woman?

From the moment he'd heard her speak with such passion the previous day, Miss Emily Beresford had emblazoned herself on his heart like letters in wet cement. How could it be that one woman of little experience in the world could share the same beliefs he'd cultivated over a lifetime? He was aware that a meeting of the minds did not necessarily equate with deep, physical appeal, but even in her appearance, Emily Beresford could not be improved upon. The very memory of her sweet face had robbed him of sleep the previous night.

What he had not anticipated was that the relationship between them would progress so rapidly. There was nothing flirtatious about her. Even when she'd kissed his hand, it was the expression of genuine emotion, the very same emotion that had prompted him to stroke her rose-petal skin.

"Do you ride in the park often, Your Grace?"

He chuckled to himself.

"What do you find so amusing?" she asked.

"I believe this is the first time I've ever come here with a woman."

Her brows lowered. "Are you not often in the Capital, Your Grace?"

"I have never missed a session of Parliament since the day I came of age."

"Then how do you explain your avoidance of Hyde Park?"

"I don't object to the park. It's most of the young women I object to. I find most of the women I've met to be empty headed and not interested in the same things that interest me."

"Then I truly am flattered that I have been so singularly honored. Little did I dream that my obsession to improve mankind would earn me the friendship of a man I so admire."

"It's I who am flattered, Miss Beresford. I believe, in you, I've actually found a woman who does not bore me."

"You ought to reserve your opinion until you know me better," she said with a nervous little laugh. "I'm sure there are those who find me and my so-called campaigns exceedingly boring."

"Thus far, I find your so-called campaigns much to my liking."

"Then the both of us, sir, must be single-mindedly boring to a large segment of the population."

He tossed his head back and laughed. "I dare say you're right, Miss Beresford. Still, I am gratified to have found a woman who shares my own interests."

"And I believe I shall enjoy the friendship of a man powerful enough to help enact some of my idealistic pursuits."

Strangely, he wanted more than friendship with this woman—which seemed oddly incongruous with his heretofore cautious approach to life. Since he'd first laid eyes on Emily Beresford, he thought less like a rational man and more like one who had been bewitched.

He turned to her. Though a proliferation of conveyances continuously passed them, he was oblivious to all. All except Emily Beresford. On this day, at this hour, she was the center of his universe. "I give you my word I will do everything in my power to earn your admiration. Sadly, I cannot control as much as I would like."

"You've done an exemplary job with your servants; now, if only your influence can carry over to those Tories who currently control Parliament."

"I vow to keep working toward that goal."

"How I wish I could pledge to help you, but, alas, women have no power."

"Next you'll be demanding to have the franchise," he said

with a laugh.

"I have more important things to work toward now, things that are attainable—unlike the franchise for women."

"And I reiterate my promise to help." By now they had ridden through the entire park and were back at the gate. Strangely, he did not want this time with her to be over. But, of course, it must. He cleared his throat. "Since you are so interested in political reform, it has occurred to me that you might like to avail yourself of my library. Even if I do say so myself, I think it may be the best outside of Oxford."

"I would love to."

"Tomorrow? You could come with your maid or one of your sisters. I wouldn't expect a maiden to come to the home of a bachelor without a proper chaperone." But he had to see her again. Soon. Even though he'd rather it just be the two of them.

"I should love to see your library."

"I'll send a carriage." He most definitely planned on collecting her himself. Knowing he'd see her the next day made parting today easier.

Chapter Three

"Do you think the duke is actually coming to escort you to his house, or is he just sending his carriage?" Lucy asked Emily.

Emily turned to her sister. "I don't know. His exact words were *I'll send a carriage.*"

"You remember his exact words?"

A soft smile transformed Emily's face. "I remember every word he's ever said to me."

Lucy's eyes widened. "I'm shocked."

"Why?"

"You're in love. I never thought it would happen."

In love? Emily hadn't put it into those words, having no experience with falling in love. The very notion stunned her. But her sister must be right. That would explain why sleep eluded her last night, why the Duke of Bentley dominated her thoughts both day and night, why she wanted to be with him every waking moment. "I believe you're right. No one's ever affected me as he has."

"I know. I do hope he comes himself to collect you."

"Why?"

"Because that will mean he's in love, too."

"You can't possibly know something like that."

"You'll see I'm right. If he comes."

As much as Emily loved her sister, she had little confidence in Lucy's assessment of things romantic. Of all the Beresford females, Lucy was the only one who had not turned down countless numbers of marriage proposals. Before she'd met the love of her life in Lord Montague, Lucy had only had one suitor, and that man had been motivated solely by Lucy's dowry. "I hope you are for I very much fear I've fallen in love with him."

"When did you two meet?" asked Lucy, her brows lowered.

"Exactly two days ago. I shall always remember it."

"And in those two days, how many times have you been together?"

"Today will be our third time—if he honors me with his presence, which I most certainly hope he does." Emily met her sister's amused gaze. "I do thank you for agreeing to accompany me today. His Grace was most insistent that my reputation be protected when I visit his house."

"I wouldn't miss it. I do hope he accompanies us for I'm positively hungering to see how he acts toward you."

A dreamy look on her face, Emily sighed. "He could not have been more attentive. Oh, Lucy, do you really think he has romantic notions toward me? I should love that above all things." She stood up from the dressing table where she'd been sitting and twirled around in front of her looking glass.

"I will be able to determine that when I see him." Lucy's voice gentled. "For your sake, I pray he does." Her gaze whisked over Emily. "You look lovely. His heart is in danger of being snared."

Emily stared into the mirror. She never saw in herself anything out of the ordinary. How she wished she could see herself as the Duke of Bentley did. Did he really think her a beauty?

Today she had dressed in ivory and, since it was another bitterly cold day, a woolen pelisse in the same shade fitted over it. At least there was nothing objectionable about her figure, though she wished she were more voluptuous. Mama always said that would come with age, so she wouldn't lament that lack now.

"Maggie did well with your hair. It's lovely," Lucy said.

"Truly?" Self-doubt was alien to Emily, but since she'd met the Duke of Bentley, she could not believe herself capable of winning the affections of so perfect a man.

"Have I ever not been truthful with you?"

"No. I can rely on you."

A tap sounded at her door. "The Duke of Bentley is here, Miss Beresford," the footman said.

He'd come himself! Exactly what she had hoped for. Her stomach flipped, her chest vibrated nervously. "We'll be right down." Her excited gaze flicked to her sister.

"You look beautiful. He'll be swept off his feet."

Exactly what Emily needed to hear.

As she descended the stairs, Lucy matching her on each step, Emily trembled. When she saw His Grace standing in the foyer looking up at her with a broad smile, she felt reassured. His smile was as comforting as sitting in front of the fire back at Tilford Hall. Without her even being aware of it, her trembling ceased.

"I'm so glad you came yourself," she blurted. Why was it her comments were so unguarded when she was with him? Not only her comments. She recalled that impulsive kiss of his hand. What must he think of her?

"I could not deprive myself of the lovely Miss Beresford's company." He eyed Lucy and smiled. "And this must be Lady Montague, your sister."

"Indeed," Lucy said.

The three of them came to stand in a circle at the foot of the broad stairway. "It appears you've saved me from having to make introductions, Your Grace," Emily said.

He bowed and kissed each lady's hand. To Lucy, he said, "I'm indebted to you for accompanying your sister. It means a great deal to me to have her peruse my library."

"I shall be happy to see it myself. Emily tells me it's the best outside of Oxford, and I, too, am rather interested in those causes promulgated by Whigs."

"I have the greatest respect for all members of the Beresford family—and their spouses. I am delighted that you Beresford beauties have all married Whigs."

In that instant, Emily vowed to also marry a Whig. Her stomach fluttered. One Whig, in particular. *If only.*

"I cannot say I married Monty because he was a Whig," Lucy admitted. "I would have married him were he a Buddhist or even a heathen I was—and still am—so much in love."

Her sister's proclamation melted something inside of Emily. How she would enjoy loving a man the way Lucy loved her Monty.

"Monty's a most fortunate man," the duke said.

"It's I who is the fortunate one." Lucy's lashes, like her voice, had lowered.

"And I am most fortunate to be escorting these two lovely sisters." He offered a forearm to each.

When he handed Emily into the waiting carriage, once again she experienced that wondrous, elevating sensation when his hand pressed hers. He took a seat opposite the sisters and proceeded to engage Lucy in conversation.

As she watched and listened, Emily found one more thing to admire about this man. His manners were impeccable, and he possessed the ability to make each person to whom he spoke feel as if their words were of monumental importance. She thought perhaps some of the duke's predisposition to admire Lucy might be linked to his admiration of her husband's parliamentary accomplishments, but, still, he could not have been nicer to the newlywed wife.

When they rounded the corner to Grosvenor Square, one house dominated the others. The duke confirmed Emily's guess that the huge mansion of Portland stone was, indeed, Bentley House. It seemed like a mighty fortress guarding the other, smaller residences there, yet, despite its size, it displayed a gracefulness like something one might find on a raj's palace nestled in India's verdant hills.

As much as she wanted to be conducted on a tour of the vast residence, she settled for being led straight past an open, soaring entryway with curving stairs straight to His Grace's scarlet library.

This room caused her to exclaim over its magnificence. A second story of books balustraded by a simple gilt railing ringed the rectangular chamber. The bookcases themselves were lined with beautifully bound leather volumes, most of them a rich red lettered with gold.

The pair of identical fireplaces at each end of the chamber added much-needed comfort on this frigid day. At one end of the chamber, a smallish crimson velvet sofa faced the fireplace, and a pair of scarlet brocade sofas faced each other in front of the other fireplace.

The two visitors followed the duke halfway across the chamber. He came to a stop, eyeing the neat rows of books in front of him. A quick scan of the titles revealed Rousseau, Paine, Bentham, Burke, and Adam Smith. After perusing the one shelf, he stood back. "The contents of this entire case, I believe, should offer any volume you care to read on progressive issues."

His glance moved from Emily to her much smaller sister. "You, too, Lady Montague, are free to borrow any of the books which strikes your fancy."

"Thank you, Your Grace, I shall be happy to avail myself of your kind offer."

Both ladies started examining the books while the duke fell back, crossed the chamber, and took a seat at his large walnut, empire-style desk where he began shuffling a stack of papers. If she wasn't mistaken, Emily thought they looked much like the papers her cousin Devere examined, papers dealing with bills being considered in the House of Lords.

Her attention returned to the shelves of writings penned by the greatest political thinkers of the day. Jeremy Bentham's newest work was among the selections. She'd been hoping to borrow her cousin's copy after his wife finished it.

But this was better. She snatched it.

Her sister was flipping through the pages of Thomas Clarkson's work on the abolition of the slave trade.

It would better suit Emily's purpose if she retained privileges here on a regular basis than to grab a stack of books now. She would relish every opportunity to come back here with the Duke of Bentley.

She turned toward His Grace, and he looked up at her. "Would it be agreeable to you, Your Grace, to allow us to each take a book today? And allow us to return when we finish so that we can select another to replace it?"

He smiled as he got to his feet and moved toward her. "It's most agreeable to me, though I wouldn't object if you wanted to take as many books as you'd like." As he came closer, he added, "I would be lying if I didn't admit it will please me even more to welcome the beautiful Miss Beresford to my home at frequent intervals. I do hope you're a fast reader."

Exactly what she wanted to hear.

HE EYED THE title of the book she'd selected. "Do not tell me you are a Benthamite?"

"I won't. While I admire Mr. Bentham a great deal, I cannot exclude individual rights."

This lovely young woman shared his own assessment of Benthamism. He'd never thought to ever find a woman who understood utilitarianism, much less one intelligent enough to select ideas from a variety of today's greatest thinkers to form her own political theories.

Miss Beresford's keen mind alone would likely not have been enough to win his overwhelming admiration, but everything about her captured his growing affection. Looking at her brought him great satisfaction, and when she smiled and her dimples deepened in that flawless face, he felt as if he'd been singled out by the gods.

Being with her was not enough, though. Being with her only intensified his desire to touch her, to feel the heat of her, to hear the clear tones of her sweet voice. It was impossible to be with her and not want to draw her slenderness into his arms. He wanted to feel his lips on hers. He wanted to possess her. He had come to believe this woman possessed his heart—the heart he'd never thought to give to any woman.

But Emily Beresford was not just any woman. This was the woman he adored. He craved her with every breath he drew.

It was imperative that he capture her affections. The memory of her soft lips on his hand the previous day had robbed him of sleep that night. Was it possible she did care about him? Could there be a greater joy on earth than possessing Emily Beresford's affections? Nothing could trump that.

He forced himself to look away from Emily and make himself agreeable to her sister. "And you, my lady, what book have you selected?"

"I've selected one to reaffirm my strong opposition to slavery. I'm happy to say Monty supports all measures to abolish the abominable practice among Englishmen."

Miss Beresford spun around to face him. "Please say you are an abolitionist."

His opinions obviously mattered to her. Strongly. He smiled down into her mossy eyes. "If you are, I must be. It seems you and I share ideas, does it not?"

She returned his smile. "Indeed, it does, Your Grace. I dare say I'm in perfect agreement with John Wesley's statement that the slave trade is *that execrable sum of all villainies*."

The more he was with Miss Beresford, the more he found to admire. The woman was remarkably well read and had a large capacity for remembering quotations from those works she had read.

But it seemed far too formal when she referred to him as *Your*

Grace. With her, he wanted something far more intimate. Ah, to hear her address him with an endearment would be blissful.

Every moment with her was blissful.

He needed to find a way to ensure he saw her every day.

And every night . . .

Chapter Four

WOULD HE, COULD he ever tire of staring at the perfection of her face? During their drive back to Piccadilly, Bentley kept having to caution himself not to stare at Emily Beresford's loveliness. To get his mind off this new-found obsession, he forced himself to converse with her sister—not that speaking with Lady Montague was a hardship. The lady was perfectly amiable and, like her sister, intelligent and well-informed on matters of government.

"I was so very proud of Lord Rockingham's speech the other day," Lady Montague said. "I believe you knew of its contents beforehand, did you not, Your Grace?"

"Oh, I did, and I most heartily approve of every word uttered." All the while he was attempting conversation with Lady Montague, he was thinking of how he could prolong the time he was spending with her lovely sister. "So, will you ladies be reading this afternoon, or do you have other plans?"

"On a day as damp and dreary as this," Miss Beresford said, "I normally wish nothing more than to indulge myself with an interesting book."

"But today?" he asked, his head cocked in query.

"I have a fitting at Madame Blanc's later this afternoon."

"If you have need of a closed-in carriage to keep you warm, mine is at your disposal."

He thought perhaps her elbow poked into her sister. "That is a most welcome offer, Your Grace! My sister—or her husband, I can't remember which—has use of their coach this afternoon, and I should love to have access to a warm conveyance. Are you sure I wouldn't be inconveniencing you greatly?"

"As it is, I'm rather floundering today. Would you object if I accompany you—and your chaperone, of course?"

"I would be delighted to have your company."

Lady Montague cleared her throat. "Actually, I believe it's Monty who's using the coach this afternoon. I'm free to chaperone. Again." Her eyes narrowed as she glared at him. "It's not proper, you know, for a man to whom one is *not* married to accompany a maiden for a dress fitting."

"Forgive me," he said. What had he been thinking? On any number of occasions, he had accompanied a ladybird to the modiste's. What was he thinking to treat the incomparable Miss Beresford as he had a bevy of mistresses? It wouldn't do at all to tarnish this virtuous young lady's reputation. He must be more mindful of her complete innocence. His only justification was that he wasn't accustomed to being around well-born maidens. "Perhaps it's best if I just send around my carriage."

Emily's face fell. She boldly met his gaze. "I do so enjoy being with you, Your Grace."

Had he imbibed an entire bottle of champagne, he could not have felt more intoxicated than he did at this moment just because of her words. He eyed her sister. "Then I would not be permitted to see your sister in the new gown?"

Lady Montague looked at her sister and shrugged. "I suppose if I'm with you, it might be permissible, but—" She turned back to face him. "Do you not think that by going to her modiste you might be signaling the wrong message? I'm sure you must know what others would be thinking."

That I'm going to marry her. "Be assured I don't want to do anything that would diminish Miss Beresford's good name."

"Then perhaps it's best you don't come with us to the dressmaker's," Lady Montague said.

Emily shrugged. "I'm sorry, Your Grace, my sister is such a stickler."

He bestowed a smile on the fragile-looking sister, then met Emily Beresford's earnest gaze. "I'm happy you're possessed of a sister who cares so deeply for your reputation."

"Thank you, Your Grace," Lady Montague said. "I don't need to tell you there are many men here in London who would like nothing more than to win Emily's hand, and I will not permit anything to destroy her chances for happiness in marriage."

"I understand. Speaking of happiness," he said, "my happiness would be unlimited if you, Miss Beresford, would do me the goodness of being my guest at Drury Lane. There's a revival of Sheridan's *School for Scandal*, and I've not a soul with whom to share my box."

"When should you like to go?" she asked.

"Alas, my engagements are scanty, to say the least. I am free for your pleasure every night." His gaze skipped to the dainty sister. "And you and Lord Montague would be most welcome."

"Monty has things scheduled every night this week—save for tonight."

"Tonight would be satisfactory to me," he said, casting a glance at Emily.

"I did have vouchers for Almack's, but I'd much rather see *School for Scandal*. I've never seen it."

His gaze traveled to Lady Montague. "Could you and Lord Montague join us tonight?"

"I think so, but I'll have to make sure Monty doesn't have other plans."

He felt like an anxious lad begging to spend the night with a friend.

When his coach pulled up in front of Montague House, Miss Beresford addressed him. "I'm looking forward to the theatre tonight. Even if Lord Montague is otherwise engaged, perhaps my other sister, Lady Churston, can accompany us. Failing that, my cousin, Harriett Rockingham, ought to be able to come."

She wants to be with me as much as I want to be with her. The lady's resolve to attend the theatre with him that night more than compensated for his disappointment over the dressmaker's fiasco.

LORD MONTAGUE WAS free to attend the theatre that night. He and his lady sat together in the duke's coach, which allowed Emily to sit beside the Duke of Bentley. Even though she had sat this close to him once before, this intimate proximity still had the power to launch frissons of excitement through her. How could this deep attraction to him continue to have such a profound—and alien—physical effect upon her? Every time his hand touched hers, her heartbeat would accelerate, her breath would hitch, and she would experience a jolt throughout her torso.

When he helped her from the coach at the entrance to Theatre Royal, she may have held his hand a second or two longer than necessary. Being with him, touching him, was becoming necessary to her. No other man would ever suit.

Though she had schooled herself to retain her pride, when she was in his presence, her resolve vanished. She feared she was behaving like all the other women who had admired him. She could not help but to acknowledge how strongly she wanted to be with him.

She wondered if she would have been this forward had he not also indicated his eagerness to be with her. Even Lucy had been aware of it.

"That man is in love with you," she had told Emily that afternoon.

Modesty almost made Emily refute the statement, but she could not. She was too desperate to believe her sister's words. "I hope you're right for I am completely and unwaveringly in love with him."

"But you hardly know him!"

"But I do. When I left Tilford, I drew up a list of all the qualities I desired in a prospective mate. I've been around the duke enough to know he possesses all those qualities—and more."

"More?"

"His dark handsomeness appeals to me greatly, and appearance was not on my list."

"What qualities were on your list?"

"Intelligence. Commitment to progressive causes. Amiability. His agreeable appearance is a plus. Much more than I'd hoped for."

"It does seem as if both of you have been snared by Cupid's arrow."

The Bentley box at the theatre was second only to the royal box, which it was closest to. Though it seated twenty, only the four of them occupied the duke's box tonight. The duke encouraged Lord and Lady Montague to sit on the front row, and he and Emily sat on the second row.

"So, you've not seen *School for Scandal* before?" he whispered as they took their seats.

"I have not, but I'm familiar with it—as well as the real personages it satirizes."

"If only Lady Melbourne were here tonight."

"If she were, all eyes would be on her instead of the stage."

"True."

As the curtain rose, the duke quietly took her hand in his.

No man had ever actually held her hand before. She was not sure how one was to act. Was it to be a quick handholding? Or did the participants continue to hold hands throughout the play? She rather hoped it were the latter for she was excessively enjoying this physical connection.

She lowered her lashes and eyed their hands. Hers looked impossibly small encased in his. Everything about this man was large. And masculine. And desirable.

As much as she had always wanted to see this play, she was

unable to concentrate on the words the actors uttered. All she could think of was how exhilarated she was, how completely she was falling in love with this man, how needy she was for this man's touch.

As thrilling as the handholding was, it awakened in her another need. She found herself thinking of an even deeper physical connection. She longed to feel his lips pressed against hers. She wanted something even more intimate than a kiss. This was the man to whom she could completely give herself. The very idea of it caused her breath to shorten.

Her thumb began to trace slow circles on the skin where his thumb joined his hand. She could tell by the change in his breathing that her actions were affecting him, too. After a few more minutes, he brought her hand to his lips for a nibbly kiss that was almost her undoing.

Then he enclosed her hand in both of his and gave no sign that he was willing to let go.

She felt as if she were a celestial being capable of flight.

When the intermission came, she feared he would ask her something about the play, the play she'd ignored for her own personal drama. Lord Montague stood and informed them that he and his wife were going to have a word with his friend, Lord Adderton.

Once they had the box to themselves, the duke turned to her, his eyes shimmering. "I have a strong desire to kiss you."

It took her a moment to respond. Should she admit she felt the same? Should she be the proper young lady and forbid such conversation? Should she tell him she had no experience kissing? Finally, she shed her pride and all but admitted to her need. "We can't here for all to see. We need a dark corner."

A slow smile stretched across his agreeable face as his gaze moved to the rear corner of the box. "I believe we've got just the place here."

She looked up into his glistening eyes and squeezed the hand that was still holding hers.

"Come, my love," he murmured, getting to his feet.

Her heartbeat exploded. He'd called her *my love*. Lucy had been right!

Still clutching his hand, she followed him into the dark corner and flowed into his embrace. It was as if their two bodies blended into one. Nothing had ever felt so good. Or so right. She slowly lifted her head. It was too dark to see him, but feeling him was even better. His mouth closed over hers, gently at first, then hungrily. Her own hunger matched his. Her lips parted, and she sucked his tongue in a magical blending. No part of her was immune from the ecstasy he gave.

It suddenly occurred to her that she had no idea what constituted a correct kiss. Was she doing it right? All she had to judge it by was her lover's reaction, and the duke seemed to be enjoying it as much as she.

He finally lifted his head and lovingly cradled her face. After dropping a kiss on her forehead, he said, "Oh, my dear Emily, I must commend the person who taught you to kiss."

"That would be you, Your Grace," she whispered.

"Ah, a natural learner." He sighed." I don't want to, but we must return to our seats."

She was still stunned over him addressing her as *my love*.

They returned to their seats, and once more he caressed her hand within both of his. "I should like to kiss you every day of my life," he whispered.

Was he proposing marriage?

Her sister and Monty returned, and the play continued. Emily knew no more about the second half than she had the first. All she could think of was one very appealing duke.

CHAPTER FIVE

RICHARD HARWOOD, THE Sixth Duke of Bentley, had always prided himself on his prudence. He never endorsed a piece of legislation until he had studied it from every angle. He was not given to extemporaneous speaking because he never spoke publicly without scripting beforehand exactly what he was going to say. And he had never made a cake of himself over any female.

Until he met Emily Beresford.

She had become his obsession. While it was true he'd only known her for less than a week, the meeting had launched four tortuous days. When he was away from her, he could not purge her from his thoughts. When he was with her, his desire to stare at her, to touch her, to possess her overwhelmed him.

When he'd left her the previous night, he'd thought that by going to Brooks's to mingle with friends and play Faro he could banish one very appealing young woman from his constant thoughts.

He'd been wrong.

The memory of the way the sweet curves of her body had molded to his, the memory of their passionate kiss and the way she had encouraged him to take her to that dark corner—their corner, he thought with torrid poignancy—intoxicated his every moment.

Alone with her in the intimacy of his box far above rows of

theatergoers, he'd said things to her he'd never uttered to any woman. He'd called her *my love*. He'd told her he wanted to kiss her every day of his life. Those words were not borne of a moment of passion. They were not words calculated to win her affections. They were the truth of his heart, a heart that had stood dormant until she brought it to vivid life.

Why was it many dozens of women over these years had failed to conquer his heart when Emily Beresford had captured it on their first meeting without even trying? Such an attraction was difficult to analyze, but if he were to try to describe why he'd fallen so thoroughly in love with her, he would have to say he loved everything about her. She might not be the perfect woman, but to him, she was.

Her beauty was only part of her allure. For years, he had repelled a great many beauties. Not one had ever captivated him as did one not-yet-twenty-year-old with soft brown hair and a dimpled smile that could illuminate the darkest night. But he thought perhaps he'd half fallen in love with her before ever clapping eyes on her. The words she'd uttered in her sweet voice had stopped him in his stride at Devere House that first day. He'd never thought to meet a woman who cared about the things he cared about. Then, when he'd seen her beauty, he'd nearly been overcome with an acute desire to possess the perfect creature.

His complete devotion to her was irrevocably finalized when she'd kissed him last night. Her purity and innocence collided with the force of their shared hunger to make it the most shattering kiss in a lifetime.

He believed her when she confessed he was the first man to kiss her, and her heated reaction told him of her strong attraction to him far more eloquently than words could have. When it became abundantly clear last night that she craved him as he craved her, he'd blurted out the closest thing to a marriage proposal that a man could have said. By doing so, he'd shocked himself. He'd never done anything so impulsive.

Throughout his sleepless night, he thought of her, longed for her.

Until that night, he'd never thought to marry. He'd almost become resigned to the idea he would be succeeded by a distant cousin because the present Duke of Bentley would never sire an heir.

But now . . . now he knew he wanted to spend every day of his life with Emily. He wanted her lying beside him every night. He wanted Emily to bear his children. He wanted to grow old with her.

As daylight sifted into his bedchamber, he came to two conclusions. First, he would beg her to ride in the park again with him that very afternoon. A day without seeing her was unthinkable. Secondly, but first in his heart, he would tell her he wanted her for his duchess.

ONCE MORE, MAGGIE was fashioning Emily's hair most becomingly. And once more, Emily was going to ride in the park with the man of her dreams. No dreams for her last night, though. She'd been far too exhilarated to sleep.

Was it because she was in bed that her thoughts kept returning to their searing kiss? Was that why she thought of how much she wanted to be lying beside him? How could one shattering kiss ignite so strumming a desire through her? As she had lain in the darkness, she throbbed for him.

She gloried in the memory of him referring to her as *my love*, and she was thrilled and perplexed over his admission that he wanted to kiss her for the rest of his days. His words fell only slightly short of asking for her hand in marriage.

Before she'd had a chance to dress for the day, His Grace sent his page with a note for her and instructions to await her reply. It was the first time she'd seen his handwriting. The neat lettering was exactly what she would have expected. Her heart soared when she read the short missive:

Unless you cruelly refuse me, it will be my pleasure to collect you for a ride in the park today—just me and the lovely Emily Beresford. Rain, fog, snow, or hail will not hinder our outing. I will do my best to keep you warm.

—Bentley

Her contemplation of just how he proposed to keep her warm sent her heartbeat hammering with pleasure.

She'd spent more than an hour readying herself for their outing. It was so frigid a day, she could not imagine many people would brave the park. She found herself wishing for a closed carriage so she could kiss him again.

She had donned her warmest dress of soft merino wool with a matching pelisse, both in a dusty rose color. An ermine muff would keep her hands warm.

As she was sitting before her dressing table while Maggie put the finishing touches on her hair, Lucy came into her bedchamber. "It has just occurred to me your duke may very well arrive in a closed carriage because of the cold weather."

Emily stiffened. She prayed her sister would not prohibit her from joining him. "It would be a thoughtful thing for him to do."

"But you cannot go alone with him in a closed carriage. Think of the scandal!"

Emily glared at her sister. She hadn't wanted to pull out her trump card, but she wasn't about to let anyone stand between her and her duke. She craved being alone with him.

"Don't glare at me like that!" Lucy admonished. "You know I'm right."

"I know all about the rules of propriety. I also know that in certain circumstances, those rules are flaunted. When you were an unmarried lady did you or did you not embark on a trip to Bath *without a chaperone* with a man you barely knew? A man who now happens to be your husband."

Lucy glared back. "But I was a betrothed woman! And, besides, Monty pledged himself to secrecy so as not to tarnish my prospects. And it wasn't as if anyone we knew ever saw us."

"No harm was done. Lord Montague fell in love with you and made an honest woman of you." Emily drew a deep breath. "Who's to see me today if we're in an enclosed coach? And . . . I may be wrong, but I sense that the Duke of Bentley means to ask for my hand in marriage. I suspect that's why he wants to be alone with me today."

Lucy squealed. Her hands clapped as she directed a huge smile at her sister. "How can you know such a delightful thing?"

"Something he said last night led me to believe an offer might be forthcoming."

"What did he say?"

Heat climbed into Emily's cheeks when she recalled him saying he wanted to kiss her every day for the rest of his life. "I'd rather not share something so intimate."

Lucy beamed at her like an indulgent parent. "I saw you two holding hands. I really believe he is falling in love with you. Monty says Bentley could have any woman in the kingdom but has never before been enamored of any of the women who idolize him."

Idolize him. "That's exactly how I feel toward the Duke of Bentley. I adore him." What had she ever done to secure the affections of so wonderful a man? How could she be so fortunate?

While it was difficult to believe a woman like she who had so little experience in the world could have stolen his heart, she believed he had, indeed, fallen in love with her just as deeply as she had fallen in love with him. The bond between them, though swiftly forged, was as permanent as the rocks at Stonehenge.

HER DUKE DID come in an enclosed carriage. When she saw it awaiting in front of Montague House, she tossed him a smile.

"You've kept your vow to keep me warm today. It is beastly cold." Her words carried on puffs of chilled air.

The firm touch of his hand helping her into the carriage sent currents of desire through her. She said not a word when he came to settle next to her in the coach.

"I did give you my word I'd do whatever it takes to keep my lovely Miss Beresford warm."

My lovely Miss Beresford. His choice of the possessive pronoun exhilarated her. Her glance fell to his lap where his leather-sheathed hands rested, and she tossed aside the muff she saw as a barrier to their handholding.

He immediately clasped one of her gloved hands. Though it was impossible to say the inside of his coach was warm, something akin to heat rushed through her when he took her hand. She smiled up at him. "You will be going to the House of Lords later today?"

"I will. There's an important vote."

"Yes, I know. On Lord Rockingham's bill to restrict child labor."

"As hard as we've worked, it hasn't a prayer of passing."

"It will one day. It's like Jefferson wrote about liberty to the Marquis de Lafayette: *we are not to expect to be translated from despotism to liberty in a featherbed*. It will take years of fighting for what's worth fighting for."

He squeezed her hand. "How wise is my Emily."

He had melted her heart again. *My Emily*. She prayed he was laying the foundation for a proposal of marriage.

Wind howled outside their carriage, and few people had come to the park on so blustery a day. He spread the rug over their laps. "I wish I could give you sunny skies and spring blooms."

"I'm perfectly happy at present, Your Grace."

"When it's just the two of us, would you do me the goodness of calling me something less formal than *Your Grace*?"

"Such as?"

"My friends call me Bentley. My mother called me Richard. Your choice entirely, my dear Miss Beresford."

A tingling sensation flicked over her. She moved her face so close to his she could feel the warmth of his breath, smell his sandalwood scent. "Richard." She had wanted to copy a page from his book and call him *My Richard* but stopped herself from doing so. She had done a pathetic job heretofore of suppressing her crippling desire for this man. She must do better at maintaining her pride.

"Now you're supposed to allow me to address you more informally," he said. "When it's just the two of us, of course."

She peered into his near-black eyes and spoke in a breathless voice. "It pleases me when you say *My Emily*."

He drew in his breath, and she could have sworn he groaned. Why did he do that?

"My Emily," he murmured in a husky voice.

To the devil with her pride! "My Richard," she whispered, her gaze never leaving his.

He gave a bitter laugh.

"What's wrong?" she asked.

"Have you no idea of the effect you have upon me?"

Her brows lowered. "I don't know what you mean."

He chuckled. "Of course, you don't. You're far too innocent for the likes of me."

She wanted to tell him she didn't want to be innocent. She wanted to be ravaged by this man she craved with every breath in, every breath out. She drew in a deep breath. "I know there is much I don't know, but I want you for my teacher." She swallowed. "I . . . am yours. To mold."

"Oh, God, Emily!" He yanked shut the coach's velvet curtain, crushed her into him, and pressed his mouth to hers. The feel of his lips sent quivers of desire racing through her. Her mouth opened to his for a searing, moist kiss that nearly overwhelmed her.

Moments earlier, she had told him she was happy. Was it

because she was anticipating the thrill of his kisses? For now, in her lover's crushing embrace, she knew it was impossible to be any happier than she was at this moment.

The courtly, well-spoken duke she thought she had come to know was something altogether different now in the throes of passion. He groaned. He held onto her as if she were a lifeline. Heat poured off his manly body.

And she loved him even more than she had moments earlier.

She totally understood his words to her the night before because she felt the very same. She wanted to kiss him every day for the rest of her life. She would never become immune to this man's physical hold on her. His every touch ignited a greedy need only he could satisfy.

Now his hands tenderly moved over her body, stirring her to heights she had never imagined. She arched into him, and he stroked and reverently fondled her breast. She squirmed, emitting a little murmur of satisfaction. Every cell in her body cried out for his possession.

When she was on the verge of begging him to make love to her, he broke away. Her lids flew open. Sweat poured from his face, and his breathing was labored. It was only then she realized she, too, was panting. Their eyes met and held.

"This won't do, you know," he said, his voice husky.

Her insides crashed. Had he not enjoyed this intimacy? Did he think her a harlot? Was he dissatisfied with her kissing? "Why?"

"Because I refuse to compromise the woman who's going to be my duchess."

It took her a moment to realize he had just proposed to her. "Me?" she asked, her voice squeaking.

"I wouldn't have anyone else."

Their eyes were still locked. Then hers narrowed. "That, my dear Richard, was not a proper proposal. Can you not say something more romantic?"

He flashed a crooked grin. "Should I tell you I love you?"

"Most definitely."

"Should I get down on bended knee and formally ask for your hand?"

"I will give you a pass on that if you do the former."

Once more, he drew her into his arms. "I love you, my Emily."

"As I love you, my darling Richard."

CHAPTER SIX

SINCE HE HAD made up his mind early that morning to ask for Emily's hand in marriage, Bentley had been torn over the decision. It could catapult him to unscaled heights of happiness—or doom him to a life of bitter regret. Marriage was, after all, forever. His doubts were fed by a lifetime ruled by carefully considered calculations. He'd never been guided by impulse.

Until he met Emily. Now, after knowing her for less than a week, he was certain he wanted to spend the rest of his life with her.

He'd been relatively confident she returned his affections and believed she would still be his for the asking several months hence. That would have given him more time to be certain she was his perfect mate. But that long a wait was intolerable. He wanted her now. His craving for her and only her blinded him to all other women. He wanted to be rid of the intense disappointment that came when had to part from her to go home to his lonely bed.

As he sat there in his coach with the most perfect being in his arms, he had never been more certain that he'd done the right thing.

"You've made me very happy," she said. "From the little I know of you, though, a hasty declaration seems most irregular—coming from you. Are you not always given to methodically analyzing something for eons before making an irrevocable step?"

He chuckled. "How is it you know me so well? I only met you a few days ago?"

"It's as the author of *Sense and Sensibility* wrote: *Seven years would be insufficient to make some people acquainted with each other, and seven days are more than enough for others.*"

Nearly every time he was with her she impressed him with the scope of her reading and the accuracy of her recall. Just another thing he loved about this woman. "For us, then, four days must have been sufficient."

She smiled up at him. "I think I knew the day I met you."

So had he. But he was too proud to own his adoration of her. He'd always thought besotted men less masculine. He wanted her to always see in him a dragon-slaying knight in armor.

"Now, my Emily, must I go to Tilford and beg your brother for your hand? He is your guardian, is he not?"

"He'll have to come to London anyway to draw up the marriage contracts. Why don't I just write to him explaining things and ask him to make haste and come to the Capital?"

"There's no chance he will turn me down, is there?"

"You do have the advantage over other men of being a duke."

"Somehow, I never felt my title attracted you."

"Then you know me well, too. Your generosity to your servants attracted me before I ever met you, but when I did—and I was already well satisfied with you because of your progressiveness and compassion—I found myself physically attracted to you. I can say it now. You're handsome."

"I'm too dark and too blasted big."

A dreamy smile softened her face. Her hand came to stroke his cheek. "I love this dark stubble on your manly face. I love your eyes. They're like chips of coal. What could be more masculine?" Her gloved hand splayed possessively on his muscled thigh, and her voice grew husky. "Your body, too, is terribly manly."

Without saying the words, he knew she craved his body as he

craved hers. He must change the conversation to something less intimate. It would not do to steal his future wife's innocence in a coach in Hyde Park.

"I beg that you dispatch that letter to your brother today. I want to marry as soon as possible."

"So do I."

"I'll procure a special license so that we can have the ceremony the minute the contracts are signed. Do let your brother know he gets whatever he wants in those contracts."

"I have a large dowry, you know."

"I wouldn't care if you didn't."

"I know."

"Where do you want the wedding to be held?"

"It seems to be becoming a family tradition to marry at Devere House. Would that be agreeable to you?"

"Of course." He couldn't help but wish it was Devere, head of the Beresford family, who was her guardian instead of her brother. How long would it take for James Beresford to arrive in London? Was there anything he could do to coax Beresford to come sooner?

Bentley's thirty years of steady patience had suddenly expired.

The skies had been darkening during the duration of their ride, and they had heard the distant rumble of thunder. Now, the clouds ripped apart and dumped on their coach like a massive waterfall. He lifted the curtain, and though it was only three in the afternoon, he couldn't see anything but darkness and pounding sheets of rain. He drew her shivering body closer. "I need to get you home."

EMILY'S BROTHER HAD once again proven that he was the best of brothers. He left Tilford as soon as he received her letter informing him of her desire to wed the Duke of Bentley, who wished to ask James' permission to make her his duchess. She had pitifully begged him to hasten to the Capital, but the fact that he'd done it so promptly earned her never-dying gratitude.

As soon as James arrived at Devere House, he sent for his solicitor and moments later asked the Duke of Bentley to join them with his solicitor. He later told his sister that of all her sisters—there were only two others—her settlements had been the easiest to draw up, owing to the duke's generosity.

"That's one of the reasons I fell in love with him," Emily admitted. "I'm so glad you approve of him."

"As illustrious as the Beresfords are, I never thought one of my sisters would snare a duke. It adds to our distinction."

She gave her brother a mock glare. "I would have fallen in love with him were he a mere mister."

"I know you turned down other high-ranking men." He smiled upon her. "And I can easily tell you're in love. Bentley's a true bang-up fellow. Even without Devere vouching for him, I would have come to the same conclusion. I shall be happy to have him for a brother."

She giggled. "Not as happy as I will be to have him for my husband."

"Are you two going on a wedding trip?"

"Yes, the morning after we wed, we shall go to Worfield Abbey." Having Richard all to herself for two weeks would be the closest thing to heaven she could ever know.

Her brother's gaze darted to the case clock on the library's mantel. "You'd best get dressed. Your bridegroom will be here in an hour."

SADLY, BENTLEY THOUGHT, he had no relations at his own wedding. His parents had not been as prolific at breeding as the Beresfords who easily filled the Devere drawing room to attend his wedding to one of their own. Chairs in the chamber had been set up on the lines of a chapel with a central aisle.

It was down this aisle that James Beresford escorted his sister. Knowing the special solemnity of the occasion and seeing her loveliness had the power to expand Bentley's heart, filling that place that had for so long stood empty.

His own beautiful Emily looked like an angel in the simple white dress she wore. It was one of those whites without a trace of ivory, just bright, chalky white like her perfect teeth. He didn't know about fabrics, but he could tell it was thin, but not so thin one could see through. The dress draped from her bosom to the floor and a bit beyond as its short train trailed her. His glance skimmed above her bosom to take in the smooth, white contour of her elegant neck and bare shoulders.

At the thought of the breasts that lay just beneath, his breath hitched. *Tonight.* Tonight all of her would be his.

She looked amazingly pretty. A ring of white flowers circled her sable-colored hair. Her lashes lowered as she moved forward, carrying a bouquet of flowers that matched her floral crown. He wasn't sure, but he thought perhaps her hands were shaking. How he wanted to draw her into his arms and reassure her that this would the happiest day of their lives.

When she looked up at him, she smiled and seemed to shed her nervousness as she came to take her place beside him. He was almost overcome by the realization that for the rest of their lives, this woman would remain at his side. Any residual doubt had long been banished. He'd never been more assured that he was doing the right thing.

He hoped she felt the same.

He took to heart every word of the wedding ceremony. He was especially moved near the end when her sweet voice shook as she said, *"I, Emily, take thee, Richard, to be my wedded husband, to have and to hold from this day forward, for better or for worse, for richer or poorer, in sickness and in health, to love, cherish, and to obey till death us do part, according to God's holy ordinance, and therefore I give thee my troth."*

He thought about the words *till death us do part* and prayed that parting would not come for many decades.

As instructed by the priest, he placed his mother's emerald and diamond ring on her slender finger and recited the words, *"With this ring I thee wed, with my body I thee worship and with all my earthly goods I thee endow. In the name of the Father, the Son, and the Holy Ghost. Amen."*

He likely did not deserve such happiness, but he was grateful for it, grateful for her, and silently vowed right here before God to cherish her for as long as he lived.

BY THE TIME the late afternoon ceremony was completed, night had fallen. All the attendees then gathered around the long dinner table in the Devere dining room to indulge in a wedding repast.

What an efficient staff Devere must employ to offer so impressive a dinner at such short notice. The Regent's own staff would have been hard pressed to match it. In addition to a never-ending supply of champagne, food offerings included turtle soup, salmon in a lobster sauce, deviled kidneys, Madeira sauce over mushrooms, olives and truffles, a magnificent round of beef, and, later, sweetmeats which included raspberry tarts and plum cake.

Devere offered the first toast. "The Beresfords heartily welcome the Duke of Bentley into our family. May he and Emily enjoy a long, happy life together."

They all swigged champagne to that. Then James offered his toast. "May my sister and her bridegroom always be as happy as they are today." His shimmering green eyes met Emily's, and he nodded his approval of this match.

Coming from a small family, Bentley was happy to now be a part of the Beresfords, who could not have been more welcoming toward him. He held each of the men in great admiration—not just because they were all conscientious Whigs, though that was a bonus to this much-wanted marriage.

Lord Rockingham was the next to give a toast. Bentley had always been a bit in awe of the young man, who was easily the most important Whig of all the men here. Rockingham cleared his throat. "I cannot express how delighted I am to welcome another Whig, a most able, dedicated Whig, to be sure, to our family. May the duke be embraced into the Beresford fold as affectionately as I have been these past few months since I married a Beresford. We are going to be a force in Parliament. Huzzah to the Beresfords!"

"Huzzah," they all said in unison, then downed another glass of champagne.

During the short time Bentley had known Emily, he'd not seen her imbibe spirits. He hoped she would be able to tolerate the large amount of champagne that was being consumed on this happy evening. This was, after all, their wedding night.

He clasped her hand beneath the table. As special as this day was and as touched as he was by the Beresfords' acceptance of him, he wished this dinner to terminate. He wanted to be alone with his wife. *My wife.* The very thought of those words gladdened his heart.

How he wanted to make love to her!

When the lengthy dinner finally ended, the Duke and Duchess of Bentley rose and moved toward the home's entry. Emily's sisters and her cousin Harriett would not let her go without embracing her and addressing her as *Your Grace*. Georgiana was the first to do so, and when she wished *Your Grace* a long and happy life with her new husband, Emily gave her a blank look, then quickly recovered. "I didn't realize you were addressing me when you said *Your Grace*. It will be some time before I can become accustomed to it."

Bentley, too, was moved. In a matter of hours, his life had become utterly complete.

ON THE COACH ride to her new home on Grosvenor Square, Emily nestled her head into her husband's solid chest and possessively settled a hand on his muscled thigh. It was impossible to be too close to this man she adored. *My husband.* Nothing to her ears had ever sounded better.

His arm came around her, and he dropped soft kisses into her hair.

"I cannot agree with Blake that those in love should not seek to say it. No, instead, I must say *Never pain to tell thy love. Love never told can never be.*" She looked up into his face. "With you, my dearest, I cannot be proud. With you, I will always be truthful, always speak my heart—which is very full tonight."

He answered her with a fiery kiss.

Then the coach rolled to a stop in front of Bentley House, and his coachman opened the door and let down the steps.

Her husband helped secure her ivory cloak before she stepped out into the misty night, and they raced to the front door. "With all the rush to get married, somehow I never found the time to show you your new home," he said.

"All I've seen is this stunning entry and your equally stunning library." Her gaze fanned over the opulent and spacious entry.

"Not *my* library. *Our* library," he said, giving her a mock scowl.

"It's overwhelming to think of this beautiful home actually being mine. I was too bashful the last time I was here to display an interest in this area. Allow me to stand here and take it all in."

The ceiling was far above, only open space soaring up three stories of curved staircase with shiny gilt railings. A multi-tier chandelier suspended over the area, its glistening crystals and rings of burning candles illuminating the large entrance as brightly as natural daylight. Even though she was from an exceedingly wealthy family, she was shocked over the extravagance. Most people saved such a costly display of candles for when they had guests visiting or for grand entertainments like balls. She would have felt worse for the poor footman charged with snuffing all these candles were it not for her certainty that he was likely the most well-compensated footman in all of London. Thanks to her generous husband.

"Does your house have a ballroom?"

His brows lowered. "*Our* house."

"Forgive me. It will take time for me to get used to being . . . your duchess." She'd never given any thought to wanting to be a duchess, and she was certain it was the man and not his title who had captured her heart. But still, she could not deny that being a duchess would be exciting.

"We do have a ballroom. It's on the top level."

Nodding, her gaze went to the floor. Another costly display. Large, alternating squares of marble in white and graphite formed a checkerboard pattern. There were no furnishings, save for a gilt sideboard to display calling cards and the day's post. She understood the need for spare furnishings so as not to detract from the classical architecture of the space.

From there, she peeked into the morning room where side chairs lined the perimeter of the small chamber.

"I don't need to see the library now," she said. "It's the most impressive home library I've ever seen. I warn you, I shall be very possessive of it."

Eyes shining, he looked down at her. "It's large enough for us to share."

They proceeded to the dinner room, another huge chamber with a table almost twice as long as that at Devere House where a dozen of them had sat for their wedding dinner earlier. The gleaming mahogany table displayed four massive silver candelabra.

"I shall look forward to hosting our first dinner here," she said. Making plans for the future together was so exhilarating.

He took her hand and moved to the door. "Let us go upstairs

now."

Family portraits climbed up the staircase wall. "Do you know who each of these ancestors are?" she asked.

"Only the ones from the last hundred years," he said with a shake of his head and a smile. "If one truly wants to know an identity, I'm told their names are written on the back."

On the first floor, he led her to the long drawing room. It, too, was lighted with a combination of candles and oil lamps to reveal butter yellow walls and silken upholstery and draperies that went well with the gilded French furnishings.

"For obvious reasons, we call this the Yellow Room." He put his hand to her elbow to steer her away and down the corridor. "Allow me to show you the duchess's chambers."

He threw open the door to what had been his mother's study. Just beyond was the bedchamber. They both featured turquoise walls, and everything about them from the silken loveseat to the bed curtains to the matching Sevres vases on the Carrara marble mantle was exquisite—and everything was in turquoise.

"Please feel free to change anything you want in here. I know it's a lot of blue, and I perfectly understand if you wish to change the color."

She giggled. "Men are hopeless with color. Only a man would call this room blue. It's turquoise." Still smiling, she shook her head. "I couldn't change a thing. These chambers are beautiful." She strolled into the bedchamber and tossed a glance at the gilt dressing table with a Venetian looking glass over it. Maggie had come earlier that day and set out all her mistress's things and had also moved her own worldly goods into her room in the servants' floor.

Emily then eyed the bed where fine silk curtains hung. Is that where she and Richard would make love? Her heartbeat accelerated.

He looked pleased as he showed her the adjacent dressing room. "And from here, you enter your husband's bedchamber." He stopped and took her hand. "The most important room. I wasn't sure how you would like your chambers, so I thought we'd sleep here in mine tonight." His voice lowered when he added, "The next Duke of Bentley might very well be conceived in this bed."

No candles burned in the duke's chamber. The only light came from a fire blazing at the hearth ten feet away from the bed that was dressed in royal blue silk.

She turned to face him, and he drew her into his arms and crushed his mouth into hers for a hungry kiss. She gloried in the feel of his hands caressing her hips, her back, then they moved possessively over her breasts.

Her breath sucked in. Her breasts felt heavy and needy for whatever he was doing to them. Quivering overtook her whole body, with a throbbing settling low in her torso. The pleasure he was giving her felt otherworldly.

With a groan, he pulled away and pressed his forehead to hers. "Will you allow your husband to help you undress?" he asked in a low, husky voice.

At that moment she would have consented to anything. Her need to be as close as possible to him, flesh to flesh, had never been greater. Her gaze not leaving his, she slowly nodded.

Before he began to disrobe her, he bent to close his mouth over her nipple, wetting the thin fabric covering it.

At that moment a loud rapping sounded at his bedchamber door. "Your Grace, I hate to disturb you, but you've just received a message that's said to be extremely urgent."

Chapter Seven

Bentley's brows lowered, and he cursed under his breath. "What the devil?" he snapped as he stormed to the door and threw it open.

There stood his valet, Shaw. "I do beg Your Grace's pardon, but the footman was beside himself about what to do with the urgent message that just came from Devere House. I took the liberty of bringing it to you myself, knowing you would likely want to see it even if it's . . ." He left *your wedding night* unsaid.

"Yes, of course." He took the missive and closed the door. At the same time, his wife, her face blanched with fear, rushed to him.

He ripped off the sealing wax and unfolded the hastily jotted note that read:

Vile thieves broke into our house and gravely injured my husband. He says it's vital that he speak with the duke at once.

—Lady Devere

Emily shrieked as she read it. "Oh, my poor cousin! We must pray for him," she managed before sobs wrenched from her.

It was several minutes before the Bentley coach was brought around, and moments later they rushed into Devere House. A solemn-looking butler told them the family was gathered upstairs.

The two of them pounded up the stairs which terminated in the spacious drawing room. James came rushing up to them, his eyes red as if he'd been crying. Beyond him was Devere's sister Harriett, who was still crying.

Emily then burst into tears. "What's happened?"

"Four masked ruffians forced their way in just after Lucy and Monty left," James began. "They rounded up all of us and stole all the coin and jewelry on our persons as they held us at knifepoint. But when they yanked away Devere's coins, the thief plunged his knife into Devere's side." James broke off, unable to say more.

"It was horrible!" Harriett said. "I feared my poor brother would bleed to death. Blood was everywhere." She broke into a fresh wave of sobs.

Emily, too, could not keep from crying. It fairly broke Bentley's heart to see her so forlorn.

"This all happened just minutes after you two left," James added.

"Thc countess's note said Devere wanted to see me." Bentley hiked a brow in query.

Harriett nodded. "Yes, he apparently said it was imperative he speak to you and my husband."

Rockingham. Devere's closest friend. Bentley was surprised that at so alarming a time his new relation was asking for him. Why not Lord Montague or Lord Churston? They'd been in the family longer than he had.

"It's a relief to know he can communicate." Bentley eyed Lady Rockingham. "Where do I go?"

"Allow me to show you to my brother's bedchamber," Harriett said. "The surgeon has been here and dressed the wound. Devere won't take the laudanum until he speaks with you, and I'm afraid he needs it badly for the pain."

"The surgeon's left?" Emily asked.

"He said he will return closer to midnight," Harriett responded. She set a hand to the duke's crooked elbow and started toward the bedchamber wing.

While flattered that Devere wished to see him at so momentous a time, Bentley was perplexed. He could not imagine why his presence would be necessary following so tragic an occurrence.

After Harriett softly knocked upon her brother's chamber door, Lady Devere—looking shaken—inched open the door, her glance darting to Bentley. "He may come in."

Harriett's lips folded into a grim line as she solemnly nodded.

Bentley came into the chamber that was illuminated by oil lamps and candlesticks on every piece of furniture that could accommodate them. Bentley supposed the surgeon had needed good light in order to stitch up the patient.

White cloth wound around Devere's torso. He lay on the bed, his arms bare, his eyes shut. Rockingham stood on the opposite side, and Lady Devere came to the bed and grasped her husband's hand. "The Duke of Bentley has come, my love."

Devere's eyes opened, and his glance arrowed to Bentley. When he tried to talk, his voice was greatly altered with weakness. "What I have to say, Caro, is only for these two men's ears." His voice was weak.

"You want me to leave the chamber?" Lady Devere asked, sniffing and trying to stifle a sob.

Her husband nodded.

Tears sliding down her cheeks, she left the chamber.

Bentley replaced her at Devere's bedside.

Devere met his gaze. "This attack on me," he started, then had to stop and take in a lungful of air. "Was made to look like a theft, but I don't think that was the aim."

Bentley looked across the bed at Rockingham to make sure he had heard his friend correctly. Rockingham's brows squeezed together as he nodded.

"You think the theft was to cover up a murder attempt?" an incredulous Bentley asked.

"Yes," Devere croaked.

"Why would anyone want to kill you?" Rockingham asked.

"I may be wrong, but I've been asking questions certain men don't want answered," Devere managed, half gasping as he tried to speak.

"Why didn't you share this with me before?" Rockingham asked.

"It's early days."

Anger flashed in Rockingham's eyes. "Early days for what?"

Devere's head turned toward Rockingham. "I hadn't told you. Some leading Tories approached me to support them in a stock scheme that sounded too good to be true."

Bentley instantly thought of the South Sea Bubble in the last century and how that stock speculation had bankrupted half the aristocratic families in England—as well as the government.

"I know that when a scheme sounds too good to be true, it usually means something's rotten," Rockingham said.

Bentley still wondered why he had been summoned here. This was troubling news, to be sure, but there was nothing he could do tonight either for it or for Devere's medical condition. Now, poor Emily would be so upset with worry over her cousin, she'd probably cry herself to sleep. On her wedding night.

Devere's gaze shifted back to Bentley. "Who are these men?" Bentley asked.

"The Chancellor of the Exchequer, for one."

Bentley nodded. "Lord Abbott." This got Bentley's shackles up. He didn't like the government speculating in risky endeavors. They could not afford to.

"Who else?" Rockingham asked.

"Lord Fletcher and Lord Sloane." Devere winced in pain.

Bentley could tell that speaking was stealing away what little bit of strength Devere had. "I take it you were approached for two reasons. First, you're one of the wealthiest men in the House of Lords . . . and you're powerful in government."

Devere's gaze flicked to Rockingham, and he spoke in a feeble voice. "Rockingham's far more powerful, but he's not a wealthy man. But you're right, Bentley." He paused a moment.

"About your speculation on why I was targeted."

Was the Bentley wealth the reason he had been summoned to Devere's bedside tonight? Now that he thought about it, he could be selected for the stock scheme for the same reasons Devere had been selected. Devere must think he could prove useful. "Targeted by those powerful lords for you to invest in their scheme or targeted by the potential murders?"

"Both," Devere said in a faint voice.

Poor fellow was losing more strength by the minute. "So you believe that because of your skepticism, they wanted to kill you to silence you?" Bentley was outraged.

Devere barely nodded.

"By God!" Rockingham cursed. "Let's go after those fiends!" He eyed Bentley.

"Can't tell anyone," Devere managed in a voice growing so faint it was barely heard. "Cannot even tell our wives. Please give me your word." His gaze went from Rockingham to Bentley and back again.

Both men vowed to stay silent about what Devere had discussed this night.

Bentley moved closer to the bed. "You do want us to investigate, do you not?"

"You, Bentley," Devere croaked. "Feign an interest in the scheme. I was supposed to meet some of them tonight at White's."

Now Bentley understood why he'd been called to Devere's bedside. Those men weren't necessarily likely to connect him with Devere, not like they would with Rockingham.

Devere turned to his friend. "I wanted you, Rock, to know so that you could help Bentley if you can, but you're to stay out of it. Stay safe." He shut his eyes tightly and with his waning breath, said, "Where in the hell is that damned laudanum?"

"He wouldn't take the laudanum until he spoke with you," Rockingham said to Bentley. "Go get Lady Devere. She'll administer it to him."

Just outside the bedchamber door, handkerchief in hand, Caroline Devere was waiting. When Bentley opened the door, she said, "Laudanum?"

Bentley nodded as she rushed into the chamber. As he stood there holding the half-open door, he took in Emily's red-rimmed eyes. "You must go home, love."

"I'll wait for you," she said.

He shook his head adamantly. He must go to White's tonight. He had to. But Devere obviously did not even want his own wife to know about this fledgling investigation, so Bentley could not share with his wife the details of tonight's meeting.

"I'm sorry." He felt lower than an adder's belly. This was his wedding night, and he wasn't going to be able to spend it with his cherished wife. "I . . . have a commission to perform for Devere which could take a considerable time." Bentley's gaze flicked to Lord Montague. "Could I beg that you see my wife home?" He loved referring to her as his wife.

Monty had been seated on a bench but leapt to his feet. "Of course, Your Grace."

All eyes—all sympathetic—went to poor Emily. Alone on her wedding night.

So much for the happiest day of his life. This was turning out pretty damned bleak. He wished to God Devere had been in good enough condition to give him more details about the worrisome stock scheme. Bentley knew nothing, but he could hardly press a man on death's door for more information.

Most importantly, he prayed Devere would recover. He was a fine man.

Once he was assured his bride had left, he, too, would leave for White's and embark on a clandestine investigation he knew next to nothing about and which could potentially put him in danger similar to that which almost killed Devere tonight.

And if that weren't bad enough, he was not permitted to explain to his bride why he couldn't be with her on their wedding night.

CHAPTER EIGHT

EMILY HAD PRAYED nonstop that her poor cousin Devere would pull through this horrid, senseless, heartbreaking injury. This was surely the worst thing that had ever happened to a member of the Beresford family. But it could have been worse. She thanked God he hadn't been killed.

A melancholy as bleak as when she'd lost her parents seeped into every cell in her body.

For in addition to her worry over Devere, she mourned that she would not be with her husband on their wedding night. She chided herself for even thinking of her own disappointment when Devere was clinging to his life, but this separation from her husband on the night of their wedding added a final layer of sadness that was difficult to dispel.

Richard had told her this would be the happiest day of their lives, and they had been on the verge of fulfilling that prophecy when they got the horrifying news about her cousin.

Also adding to her disappointment over the separation from her husband was his failure to communicate with her. She was crushed that Richard had not taken her into his full confidence about what had transpired at Devere's sickbed. After all, wasn't that was marriage was about—being truthful and open with one's life partner? Surely this wasn't a portent of what kind of husband he was going to be. Surely she could not have been that wrong about him.

She was uncommonly perplexed as to why her cousin wanted Richard at his bedside. Richard had only joined their family that same day. Devere had not wanted his sister or his cousins, or even the other husbands of his female cousins, Lord Montague or Lord Churston, in his sick room. Just Richard, along with Lord Rockingham, whom everyone knew had been Devere's closest friend since childhood.

If Devere were being given laudanum just as Richard told her to return home, her cousin wouldn't be needing her husband for hours—the laudanum was supposed to render him unconscious. What, then, was Richard planning to do tonight? Why could it not have waited until morning? How could he abandon her on their wedding night? She knew he had looked forward to their wedding night with the same eagerness as she. Why, then, had he forsaken her?

She moved across her bedchamber and rang for Maggie. Earlier in the day, she had dismissed her maid, believing that on this night it would be her husband, and not her maid, who would help her undress. Now, though, she needed Maggie.

When her maid entered her bedchamber, Emily shrugged her shoulders, a forlorn look on her face. "My husband was called away because my poor cousin, Lord Devere, was almost killed. It seems I will need your assistance after all in preparing for bed."

"Well, if this ain't the worst wedding night I ever heard of!" Maggie walked over and began to unpin her mistress's hair. Then she helped Emily out of her gown and underclothing and assisted her into a sheer linen night shift. Emily stole a glance into her looking glass to try to see herself as Richard would, were he here. She had looked forward to sharing such intimacy with the man she loved.

"What a pity His Grace ain't here," Maggie commiserated. "When do you expect him?"

It pained Emily to admit her husband had omitted to share that detail with his bride. "I don't know."

After Maggie left her, Emily took the copy of the Bentham book she'd been reading and went to her husband's bedchamber. He had told her they would sleep here on their wedding night, and she meant to do just that. It was her best hope of making love with her husband.

The oil lamp by one side of the bed had now been lighted. Her plan was to read until Richard came home. Then, perhaps, they could continue what they had begun when the wretched news about Devere had shattered everything. Just the memory of her husband's hands on her breast awakened her to a strumming need. But she mustn't allow her thoughts to go there, not when Richard wasn't here. It would be far too painful a loss to contemplate.

She pulled back the velvet bedcovering and climbed atop the huge bed, propping herself up on a mound of pillows as she opened her book and began to read.

Even after the anxious time spent with her brother, her sisters, and cousins at Devere House, she still felt the effects of the large quantity of champagne she had imbibed earlier that evening. Now, all alone with no one to engage with, she realized the champagne was making her groggy. The presence of others had kept her alert, but she was fading fast now. This was far earlier than her normal bedtime, yet she was far sleepier than she was at her normal bedtime.

I must stay awake. She fully intended to be alert when her husband returned and to have this be their proper wedding night in spite of the tragedy that had occurred. She forced herself to continue reading, alternating each passage with a prayer for her cousin Devere.

Unfortunately, her face kept plopping on top of the pages of the open book. Finally, after half a dozen tries, she gave up, turned off the oil lamp, and sank into a deep slumber.

WHEN BENTLEY ENTERED White's, he had hoped to find the Chancellor of the Exchequer there, but there was no sign of Lord Abbott. While Bentley normally strolled through the warren of rooms in search of fellow Whigs—an uncommon occurrence at this bastion of Tories—tonight he wished to ingratiate himself with some powerful Tories, namely Lords Fletcher and Sloane.

He was in luck. Not only were those two men at White's, but they were seated at a long table in the dinner room, a place where it would not arouse suspicion if Bentley joined them to partake of a meal.

What a pity he was so full from his impressive wedding dinner. Nevertheless, he would force himself to dine here.

He was even fortunate enough to be able to sit next to Lord Fletcher, a man some two decades Bentley's senior. Because the little bit of hair left on Fletcher's head was a steely gray, he looked even older than his chronological years.

"Good evening, Your Grace," Fletcher greeted. "We're not accustomed to seeing you dine here."

"It pains me to say I haven't been satisfied with the food at Brooks's as of late. I dare say they must have a new chef. And . . ." Bentley had decided to throw out the name of another powerful Tory who could generally be found at White's. "Lord Babbington highly recommended to me the food here."

As a waiter brought his wine glass, Bentley hoped to God these men had no knowledge that he'd married that very day. Nothing could arouse more suspicion than a bridegroom deserting his beautiful wife on their wedding night to go to a club that was not his usual haunt. Fortunately, Bentley had kept the details of his nuptials private, and he believed Emily had shared their marriage plans only with her family.

"Lord Babbington's right," said Lord Sloane, who sat on the other side of Lord Fletcher. "It's good to see a staunch Whig like you here, Your Grace. Perhaps we can sway you to our side."

Lord Sloane was somewhere between the age of Bentley and Lord Fletcher, which would put him around forty. And while he was fairly prominent in Parliament, his biggest interest was in his impressive stable. The man was more likely to be at a race meeting than a session of Parliament.

Bentley shrugged. "I don't know how staunch I am. I like to think of myself as voting for what I think is right, whether it be proposed by a Whig or a Tory."

"Well spoken, Bentley." Lord Fletcher said as the waiter brought Bentley a plate of steaming food.

Bentley sipped his wine before speaking again. "So, what did you gentlemen think of Rockingham's speech?"

The two Tories eyed each other, and Lord Sloane smirked. "Rockingham is a fine fellow, a champion of the downtrodden," Lord Fletcher said.

"But, while his ideas are noble, we are unable to fund his ambitious proposals. You understand the war has been very costly, and our coffers are empty."

"I do understand that," Bentley said. "A pity we can't think of a way to replenish the government's funds without increasing taxes." He hoped these gentlemen would pick up on his conversational gambit.

"A man of your considerable wealth must know a thing or two about amassing and retaining that wealth," Lord Fletcher said.

Which way should Bentley go here? Should he present a shrewd persona, or should he act as if he needed guidance in the area of amassing fortune? He gambled on the latter. After all, if these men were involved in a risky scheme, they would need support from other wealthy men like him, men with access to large sums of money, men who might be foolishly influenced.

Bentley shrugged. "My strength lays in listening to others who know more about amassing fortunes than I do."

Fletcher's gaze flicked to his companion. "Perhaps tomorrow you could join us and some other investors to discuss an exciting new proposition we believe could prop up our country's failing coffers—as well as our own."

"I'm always eager to increase my fortune," Bentley said. It was a lie, of course. Since his personal wealth was so excessive, he was more interested in using it to improve the lives of those who toiled for him than in amassing a larger fortune. A man could only do so much, and he preferred to spend his time bettering others' lot than in cushioning his own.

He smiled to himself as he thought again of the woman he'd married whose ideas so closely mirrored his own. In his Emily, he had, indeed, found the perfect woman for him.

Though he lacked any appetite, he mustn't allow these men to know he'd already eaten, so he dug into his turbot in French sauce. "Well, it seems Babbington's right about the food here. This is the best turbot I've had in an age."

"We do have an excellent chef here," Lord Sloane conceded.

"Yes, I understand he's French," Lord Fletcher added.

Bentley put another bite in his mouth and made appreciative noises. "Well, that explains it. They're the best."

After they finished eating, the two men invited Bentley to join them in a game of whist. They played for two hours before saying their farewells and agreeing to meet at Lord Fletcher's the following night. "We have much to do in Parliament tomorrow," Lord Sloane added.

Bentley was weary as he made his way home to Grosvenor Square in the wee hours of the morning. He found himself thinking about the vicious attack on Devere. Could one of those two men he'd been with that night be responsible for ordering the earl's death? The very idea sickened him.

He also found himself silently praying for Devere's recovery.

Mostly, he thought of his beloved bride. He could still hear the solemnity in her sweet voice when she'd recited her wedding vows that afternoon.

After he reached his house, climbed the stairs to his bedchamber, and opened the door, he stopped, shocked to see that his wife was soundly sleeping in his bed.

His heart softened as he took in the beauty of his precious

Emily nestled in his bed, her sable hair fanning on the pillow, much of her creamy flesh exposed beneath the fine linen night shift. At any other time, seeing this woman like this in his bed would have driven him mad with want. Tonight, though, he was too exhausted to entertain thoughts of making love.

Which was a good thing, considering that he would never awaken his wife to satisfy his own pleasure.

He quietly shut the door behind him and stood there gazing at her as she lay bathed in the fire's dimming light. He swelled with a heady sense of possession toward this woman who had stolen his heart.

He shed his clothing and eased into the bed beside her, lamenting that they'd not experienced a proper wedding night. Even this coming night, he must be away from her again. For Devere's sake. It was imperative he learn who was responsible for the near-fatal injury to his wife's cousin.

He drew in a deep breath and inhaled the scent of roses. Emily's scent. There was something incredibly comforting about lying here beside his wife, listening to the steady rhythm of her breathing and feeling a peaceful contentment he'd not have thought possible earlier in the evening as he'd stood at Devere's bedside.

It would be best for the purposes of Bentley's present inquiries if no one in London learned that he had married into the Beresford family, that he was now related to the Earl of Devere. Not when the earl was the target of a murder plot. Who else close to him might be targeted?

He dreaded telling his bride that they would not be able to acknowledge the wedding. Not until he learned who ordered the murder of Devere.

And he couldn't tell his wife why they couldn't acknowledge their marriage.

If he weren't so damned tired, he could weep.

Instead, he fell into a deep sleep.

CHAPTER NINE

THE SUN WAS high in the sky when Bentley finally awakened at noon. His first thought was of Emily. She was in his bed. He quickly spun around to face his wife, but she was no longer lying beside him. Disappointment crashing through him, he propped himself up to scan the chamber for her. Not seeing her, he sighed while cursing himself for sleeping away his day and not sharing it with Emily. Now he would have to hurriedly dress to attend Parliament.

Another separation from the woman he loved.

He rang for Shaw. He'd previously told his valet his services would not be needed on his wedding night or the morning afterward. Bentley had envisioned Emily seductively wrapping him in a cravat the morning after a long night of lovemaking. With agonizing impatience, he'd also looked forward to removing Emily's attire, piece by revealing piece on their wedding night.

But fate had certainly intervened to thwart his best-laid plans, but not as cruelly as fate had dealt with poor Devere. Before he went to Parliament, Bentley would stop off at Devere House to see if his wife's cousin had shown any improvement.

It would also be helpful if Devere could shed a bit more light on the situation with the stocks. Bentley's lack of information made him feel as if he were fencing while blindfolded.

When Shaw came, the discreet servant said not a word about Bentley's uncompleted wedding night.

Bentley cleared his throat. "Do you know, dear fellow, where the duchess is this morning?"

The valet hesitated a moment before attempting an answer. "Her Grace, along with her maid, has been overseeing the . . . reapportionment of her luggage. She's—if I might be so bold as to say so—she's been dabbing at her eyes with a handkerchief and is subject to wailing."

Poor Emily. She must be distraught over Devere. There was also the disappointment that they would no longer be able to take a honeymoon trip to Worfield Abbey. Those two things were enough to make anyone cry.

It suddenly occurred to Bentley that Shaw might not understand the source of the duchess's melancholy. Surely, the valet didn't think her wedding night activities had been so unsatisfactory they had caused the new duchess such extreme distress.

"My bride has good reason to cry," the duke defended. "Her cousin, the Earl of Devere, was gravely wounded last night. Because of that, she has been denied a proper wedding night as well as a honeymoon."

"Most distressing, indeed, Your Grace." Shaw squatted down to help his master put on his boots. "Now, if Your Grace would care to stand, I shall attempt to do justice to your cravat."

After he was fully dressed, Bentley went through the connecting dressing rooms and came out in his wife's bedchamber. She bent over a valise on her bed, tossing out dresses and instructing the maid next to her to see to their care.

"Good morning, my beautiful duchess," he greeted.

She spun around to face him. Even though her eyes were rimmed in red from her recent crying, she was still the prettiest woman he'd ever seen. "You finally awakened! What time did you get in, my darling? You were sleeping like the dead, and I hated to awaken you."

Anyone listening would think they were a long-married couple. She spoke like one who had no secrets from her spouse. A pity he had to keep secrets from her. It was a pity, too, that she hadn't awakened him. He regretted that missed opportunity to wake up in the morning with his wife beside him. "Forgive me for sleeping so late. It was nearly dawn when I finally got home."

Emily faced her maid. "You may go now, Maggie."

At least they would have a few private minutes before he had to leave. He dreaded what he had to tell her now, when she was already in such a bleak mood.

He moved to stand behind her, his arms encircling her, his mouth pressed close to her ear. "I'm so sorry we'll not be able to take that wedding trip. I don't think either of us could consider leaving until we see improvement in your cousin."

"I agree."

"I'm sorry, too, we had no wedding night together."

She sniffed and dabbed at her eyes. "It's wretchedly selfish of me to even think about my own thwarted hopes when my poor cousin is clinging to life." That comment elicited a fresh wave of cries.

He drew her closer and murmured. "Have you heard how he's doing today?"

"I sent a note around this morning, inquiring, and was told he's non-respons—" She could not finish as sobs wrenched from her.

"Let us go to Devere House straight away. Perhaps he's taken a turn for the better now."

On their way to her cousin's, he broached the subject he dreaded more than anything. It would have been so much easier to explain were he permitted to be open and honest with her, but he'd given Devere his word. "A matter has come up of grave importance that makes it imperative that—for a short time—we will not be permitted to acknowledge our marriage because it's possible . . ." *It's possible such knowledge might put them in danger.* However, he was not permitted to tell her that. At this time.

She spun around and glared at him. "What's possible?"

"I am not at liberty to tell you just now."

Her eyes filled with tears. "Do you regret marrying me?"

He solemnly shook his head. "Never that."

The lines of her mouth thinned as she went rigid and did not speak to him the remainder of the drive.

HOW SELFISH EMILY was to be wallowing in self-pity over her own marital disappointment when Devere was fighting for his life! None of her relatives now gathering at Devere House needed to know of the crushing discord in her marriage. Each of them already appeared to be as melancholy as she. Every member of the family—save for those residing in Vienna—was there: her brother, both her sisters and their husbands, her cousin Harriett and her husband, as well as Devere's wife. Poor Caro Devere refused to leave her husband's side. The others had offered to spell her while she got some sleep, but she refused.

A bitter sadness settled over every member of the Beresford family.

"Has my cousin awakened from the laudanum?" Emily asked Harriett.

Her eyes welling with tears, Harriett shook her head.

"What does the surgeon say?"

Harriett started to answer but collapsed into tears. Her husband rushed to put his arm around her and finish: "The surgeon said he didn't want to give false hope. These kinds of injuries can heal with a complete recovery—or they can become infected with no chance of survival."

Sobs broke from Emily, and Richard rushed to crush her to him. In spite of her sorrow, it felt wondrous to be held in her husband's embrace. She clung to him as she wept. She wept for Devere, and she wept for her own unrealized dream of being happily married to Richard. Why was Richard asking her to deny their marriage? Why had he deserted her on their wedding night?

Georgiana addressed Rockingham. "Why did Devere want to talk to you and the duke in private last night?"

Leave it to her sister to demand a frank explanation.

Rockingham shook his head. "Just a private parliamentary matter."

"Then why didn't he speak to Charles and Monty, too?" Georgiana demanded. "They're good Whigs."

"It didn't concern them," Lord Rockingham said.

"What did it concern?" Harriett asked.

"Nothing of import." Rockingham's gaze snapped to Lord Montague. "We won't be of any use here today. We can accomplish more if we go on to the House of Lords now."

"Yes," Richard added. "There's an important vote today on the Civil List."

Harriett whimpered. "Do go on, love. I'll send for you if there are any . . . developments with my brother."

"There's just one thing I need to mention," Richard said, still with an arm around his wife as his gaze circled the group. "For a short time, it's best that we not mention yesterday's wedding. Let's not yet refer to my wife as the Duchess of Bentley. I have strong reasons for this. I'll explain later, when Devere is improved."

Harriett's startled gaze locked with Emily's, and she shrugged.

I must not cry. Color hiked into Emily's cheeks. She was humiliated. Why was her husband disavowing their marriage? He'd said he didn't regret marrying her, but he must. She forced an insincere smile and shrugged. "It will be just for a short time." For reasons her husband refused to share with her.

This marriage was not starting off at all properly. She'd never been so disappointed.

"Shall we go, gentlemen?" Lord Rockingham asked.

"A word with my wife first," Richard said. He took her hand and asked her to see him to the door. When they reached the bottom of the stairs, he turned to her and clasped both her hands. "It pains me to tell you not to wait up for me tonight. An important matter having to do with Devere will keep me away again tonight."

"What matter?"

His lashes lowered. "I am not at liberty—"

"To say."

Sadness shone in his dark eyes when he looked at her. "Will you kiss your husband goodbye?"

Tears now streaming down her face, she shook her head. "I think not."

His thumbs brushed away her tears, and he looked as melancholy as she felt. She doubted, though, his heart hurt as badly as hers. If it did, he wouldn't have been able to inflict such pain on her.

BENTLEY KNEW HE'D hurt his wife. Were Devere not at death's door, he could curse the man for putting him in such an untenable position. Seeing the melancholy on Emily's face and not being able to relieve it was as bad as watching her flounder on an angry sea and not be able to help her.

Only yesterday he'd vowed before man and God to love and cherish her until they were parted by death, and now he was asking her to disown her status as his wife. What a pity he could not tell her he was doing this to protect them from whoever it was who made an attempt on Devere's life.

Devere hadn't wanted anyone to know of his suspicions. It was best, after all, to allow the one responsible for the murder attempt to believe no one suspected foul play. That person must never suspect Bentley of being in league with Devere. Or married to a member of Devere's illustrious family.

Perhaps tonight he would find out who wanted Devere dead.

Chapter Ten

Bentley had expected the Chancellor of the Exchequer, Lord Abbott, to be at Fletcher's house on Portman Square that night, but he was not there when he arrived. Perhaps he would come later. Since his name was the first one Devere had mentioned last evening, Abbott must be integral to this stock scheme—the scheme about which Bentley needed to learn.

The Fletcher butler showed him to a library richly paneled in walnut. Several men were already there, seated around the hearth on a pair of sky-blue sofas and an assortment of wooden armchairs.

Bentley recognized every man. All were Tories, and all served in the House of Lords, save for the exceedingly wealthy Thomas Cookson, a young man who recently won a seat in the House of Commons and who Bentley knew only by sight.

The gentlemen stood to greet him when he entered the library. "Ah, the Duke of Bentley!" Lord Crawford stepped forward to shake his hand. "We are delighted that you've come tonight."

"Indeed, we are," Lord Livingston concurred as he, too, shook Bentley's hand. Livingston had been at Eton when Bentley was there. He was a leading Tory, and Bentley had always found him to be a man of integrity. There's no way that Livingston, under any circumstances, would ever condone the attempt on Devere's life.

After exchanging pleasantries with the seven other men there, Bentley sat in a high-backed Tudor armchair.

Lord Sloane was anxious to get back to the tale of his prized filly, a direct descendent of the Godolphin Barb (a fact Sloane never failed to mention), coming from behind to win the Derby at Epsom Downs.

That discussion then led to a volley of queries about Sloan's stables, said to number 300 horses, and the sterling reputation of his studs.

"Your father, may he rest in peace, is to be commended for establishing what's become the finest stables in England," said Lord Stanbridge.

"Indeed he is," the son agreed, "though I've made it my life's work to carry on where he left off, and I'm proud to say, we've won more Derbies under my oversight than during my father's lifetime."

Modesty was not one of Sloane's virtues, Bentley thought. In fact, it would be far easier to imagine Sloane ordering the murder of Devere than to suspect any other man here. Though, Bentley had to admit, the thought of any of these men being a callous murderer was difficult to believe.

Once all the talk of horses died down, their host, Lord Fletcher, tried to redirect the conversation to the matter of the stock scheme. "I believe the Duke of Bentley has come here tonight to learn about the exciting opportunity to be in the formative stages of the New Londinium project."

Now Bentley had a name. His brows hiked.

"We may have lost one of our best potential investors," Lord Nicholson said.

All the men in the chamber looked at Nicholson, quizzing expressions on their faces.

"I've just learned that Lord Devere was gravely injured during a bold theft that occurred at his home last night."

Judging from the men's reactions which ranged from sputtered oaths to gaping mouths, Devere was a great favorite.

Bentley wasn't sure how he should react to the news. What if someone in this chamber knew that his nuptials had been held at Devere House yesterday? He decided a show of concern should suffice. He certainly was not about to volunteer that the family had gathered there to celebrate his wedding. If anyone here in this chamber knew about his marriage, it was bound to come up now. If it did, he would not deny it.

Lord Crawford looked stricken. "How in the devil did that happen?"

Lord Nicholson, shaking his head woefully, continued. "Some sort of family gathering was held at Devere House early in the evening last night—I suspect a dinner—when knife-wielding ruffians broke into the house and demanded jewelry and coin from all who were there. I dare say the thieves must have made out quite well. Especially from the jewelry those Beresford women wear."

Lord Fletcher nodded. "The Beresford wealth is significant."

The statement was supported with nods from the men gathered there.

Lord Nicholson went on, "From what I learned, when the thieves reached Lord Devere, they must have become very impatient for they stabbed him in the heart before stripping him of his jewels and coin."

As rumors tend to do, this one strayed from the truth. Thank God Devere's stab wound missed his heart. It hit too close as it was. But this version of the robbery did fire up sympathies for his wife's cousin.

"Then he's dead?" Cookson asked, his face collapsed in concern.

"No," Nichols answered. "He's fighting for his life."

Bentley paid particular attention to the way the other men reacted to the news of Devere's plight. To a man, each of them took the news with shock, dismay, and concern for Devere's recovery.

"Good lord!" Lord Stanbridge said, "It could have happened

to any of us. I, for one, will have my servants be more diligent about locking all our doors and windows."

Cookson, who was recently wed, shook his head. "I never thought that presenting my wife with lovely jewels might jeopardize her life. I'm going to ask that she curtail the wearing of her jewels only for truly special occasions. This is horrifying."

"It truly is," Lord Livingston said. "And to think, it happened in his own house!"

"One would think a man as wealthy as Devere might be better protected," Lord Sloane said.

"I imagine he will in the future," Bentley said, his voice morose, "if he survives, which I pray he does."

Bentley's stomach had been tied in knots during the discussion about Devere. Had his marriage been mentioned, it would have made his presence in this group more difficult. That his marriage was never mentioned offered him a measure of relief.

"It's the Beresford family wealth that encouraged us to ask Lord Devere to participate in our project," Lord Fletcher said. "We need men of wealth and—" He eyed Bentley. "Men of exalted rank will help us recruit other men looking to expand their wealth. We could certainly use a duke in a group."

"That would be as good as gold for us in our adverts," Nicholson added.

"Just what is this New Londinium offering?" Bentley asked.

"Allow me to explain," Fletcher continued. "During the last century, Captain Cook discovered a small island off the coast of South America. He called it New Londinium. The island's only inhabitants consisted of a small group of indigenous people Cook was not able to communicate with. His writings, though, commented on the large amount of gold jewelry these people wore. Cook believed there was a gold mine on this island, but because of the wretched weather conditions during his visit, his men were prohibited from locating it, and he had other obligations that had to be met, forcing him to leave.

"Our group is being formed to colonize the island and take

control of mining and exporting all gold found there," Fletcher said.

"Yes, according to Captain Cook's notes," Lord Sloane said, "he had hoped to form an expedition to come back one day for the purpose of mining, but his murder put a stop to those plans."

Just as Devere's murder might have stopped him from thwarting their scheme.

"That sounds interesting," Bentley said. He was thinking how he needed to see if his library had a copy of Cook's journals. One way or another, he would get his hands on them and read the accounts for himself. But he dare not alarm the investors with his distrust. That must have been what accounted for Devere's expendability.

"It's not only interesting," Fletched said, "but it's got the potential to make vast fortunes."

"So, since this is presumed to be a British colony, I suppose our government will have a stake in this endeavor," Bentley said.

"That is our hope," Fletcher answered.

"Is Lord Abbott agreeable to participation?" Bentley asked.

Lord Sloane nodded. "He is, but the authority does not rest solely with him. It's vital that we get other powerful men, men like you, to go along with the plan."

"I cannot stress strongly enough how important it is to have a list of supporters that includes names like the Duke of Bentley," Nichols said. "We've also been trying to enlist the patronage of at least one of the royal dukes."

"Forgive my ignorance," Bentley began. "I don't normally deal directly with these stock matters. I employ men who know a great deal more than I. My question is, we cannot actually list the royal dukes as benefactors to this cause unless they actually put up their own money, can we? In other words, we are not permitted to bribe them with shares in exchange for their patronage, are we?" As soon as he asked the question, he regretted it. Was he following the type of inquiry that resulted in the attempt on Devere's life?

He could have gleaned that information from other sources. He should not alienate the men in this chamber. One of them could turn out to be the one who ordered Devere's death.

Lord Fletcher shrugged. "Like you, Your Grace, I am not that knowledgeable about the legal constraints with setting up shares and all, but we will certainly have a man attend to all of that for us."

Will? Why did they not already have such a man in place? Was this the kind of inquiry that resulted in the plan to kill Devere? Bentley was not sure how many questions or what type of questions to ask. He wanted to seem interested but not negatively so. He wanted to know the answer to the question about having a man look into all the legalities of the stock shares but dare not ask.

If Devere tried to explore the issues that caused Bentley consternation, it could explain what happened to him.

He thought of a safe question. "Tell me, what kind of annual percentage could we expect to see on an investment?"

"We're starting with a promise of six percent and hope to increase that as the company gets established," Lord Fletcher said.

Bentley's brows rose. "Six percent is a very handsome return."

As the men spoke, Bentley kept eyeing the case clock upon the mantelpiece, fervently hoping he would be able to make it home in time to go to bed with his wife. But the men, going through several decanters of brandy, kept asking more questions and sidestepping into other matters.

It was after two before he could leave. And then it would be too late to join his wife.

UNLIKE ON THE previous night, Emily chose not to sleep in her husband's bed the second night of their marriage. Truth be told, she was out of charity with her husband. Each memory of how her husband had hurt her stirred up a fresh wave of anguish, yet no matter how shabbily she had been treated, she was still desperately in love with the man she had married.

She had spent the day with her siblings and cousins at Devere House. They were all, naturally, worried about Devere. The brightest spot in their day occurred when he awakened, but since he was in so much pain, they'd been forced to administer more laudanum. As long as he was able to awaken and to speak, they were optimistic he would recover.

They were also delighted that no signs of infection had developed. "It will take time," the surgeon reassured them. He was much more hopeful than he'd been the previous day, which helped to lift their sagging spirits.

It was a testament to how beloved Devere was that James had continued on in the Capital when he longed for Tilford. His strong devotion to its cattle and agriculture had become the driving force of his life.

Emily wished her brother could find a nice wife and start a family, but who was she to deem what was best for him? Her love and devotion to one particular man was making her miserable.

After dining at Devere House, the Montague coach dropped her off at her new home on Grosvenor Square. She knew Richard would not be home at this early an hour. Lords Montague, Rockingham, and Churston had only just finished a long session of the House of Lords, and she knew Richard had other plans after Parliament. Plans he was not at liberty to divulge to her.

His absence, coupled with his failure to consummate their marriage, was beginning to torture her with doubts. Had he been involved with a ladybird before they met? Was he in love with the ladybird? Would Emily's own lovemaking not satisfy like that with an experienced . . . lover?

Those thoughts left her miserable.

She determined to wait up for her husband this night. But not in his bed.

She would be able to hear him when he returned home. Then she would stroll casually into his bedchamber in the hopes of igniting his passion.

Maggie assisted her in dressing prettily for bed. Then, armed with her Bentham book, Emily climbed on top of her bed and began to read by the light of the nearby oil lamp. Every twenty or thirty minutes she consulted the clock on her mantelpiece. The last time she looked, it was one o'clock. Soon thereafter, she fell asleep.

IT WAS HALF past two when Bentley finally made it home. It was too much to hope that Emily might still be awake. He went first to his bedchamber. Seeing the empty bed gave him a sinking feeling. Not finding her there was every bit as disappointing as when his bride had refused to kiss him earlier that day.

This investigation Devere had charged him with was destroying his wife's love—and their marriage.

There was nothing he wouldn't do for Emily, but when a gentleman gave his word—as he and Rockingham had done with Devere—he was bound to honor it even at a mounting personal cost.

Hungry just to cast his eyes on his wife, he quietly went to her bedchamber. His hopes rose when he saw the oil lamp was on, but he deflated as soon as he saw that she'd gone to sleep, an open book dropped beside her.

He stood there a moment, looking at her, a gnawing hurt in his heart. She was as lovely and pure looking in her sleep as she was when awake. More so, even, he thought as his gaze went from her sweet face with down-swept dark lashes feathering against pink cheeks to the silky skin on her exposed shoulders. An indefinable quality in her could only be captured by one of those Italian masters who painted the Madonna with Child. His wife possessed that same feminine innocence.

Though there was nothing remotely seductive about her in sleep, he'd never wanted anything more than he wanted this woman at this moment.

With a sinking sense of disappointment, he strode to her bedside table, extinguished the lamp, and left the chamber. When would he ever get to make love to his wife?

CHAPTER ELEVEN

SHAW INFORMED BENTLEY that the duchess had left much earlier that morning to go to Devere House. Some marriage this was! He had longed to awaken each morning to find his lovely wife lying beside him, but not once since they'd married had that occurred.

After he dressed for the day but before he went to Devere House, Bentley had to pursue an avenue of inquiry in his library. It took him several minutes to locate what he was looking for: journals of Captain Cook. He knew Cook had undertaken three voyages, but only journals of the first voyage were in his possession. Bentley's late father must have read this, but this was the first time Bentley had opened either of the two volumes chronicling the journey of the Endeavour, which began in 1768.

In the first volume, Bentley found what he was looking for. The first thing he examined was a map of the island Cook had named New Londinium. According to the scale, the island was only four miles long and under two miles wide. It seemed to Bentley it was too small to be significant. No landmarks showed on Cook's map, and certainly nothing to indicate a gold mine.

Bentley then set about to read about the island. Apparently, Cook's crew was there during a storm that sounded suspiciously like a hurricane. Because the weather was characterized by fierce winds and driving rains, the men were prohibited from leaving the ship. At one point, Cook feared the winds would slam the *Endeavour* against rocks, which would destroy the vessel beyond the possibility of repair. Cook despaired of ever again seeing his wife and young children.

From their spyglasses, Cook and his crew were able to observe the natives as they were attempting to secure their fragile housing against the damaging winds. That was when they first observed that the men were adorned with what appeared to be large quantities of gold.

Bentley eagerly read on to see when Cook confirmed the presence of gold. He read every entry, but once the weather cleared, Cook ordered the expedition to continue on in their quest to find the continent of Terra Australis.

That passing reference to gold was the only mention of the precious metal. Not once in his journals did Cook ever even speculate that there might be a gold mine on the island.

Would Cook have any interest in returning to the insignificant island on one of his future voyages? If only the Bentley library had all of Cook's journals. How could Bentley get his hands on the other journals? If anyone in London had them, surely it would be retired Admiral Lord Hawthorne.

Just as Bentley was determining to go around to the admiral's house on Piccadilly, he realized he could not take the chance of going himself. He could not risk the members of the New Londinium scheme learning of his skepticism. He would have to send another trusted man.

Rockingham. He was the only man who could undertake the mission. Bentley knew he'd find Rockingham at Devere House this morning.

All members of the Beresford family currently residing in London were gathered at Devere House, including Bentley's own pretty duchess. After he climbed the stairs to the Devere drawing room, it gladdened his heart to cast his gaze upon his wife. "Good day to you, Your Grace," he said, smiling at Emily.

She offered him a shy smile in return. She looked lovely—and incredibly young—dressed in pale pink. As much as he wanted to chide her for not staying at their home to share breakfast with her new husband, he knew that because of Devere's frightful injury, these were not normal times. He fully understood her worry over her cousin. Indeed, everyone crowded in this chamber worried about Devere.

He strolled to his wife and brushed his lips across her silken cheek. "How is your cousin today? Any improvement?"

"Caro thinks so, but it's very slim. He's still on heavy doses of laudanum."

He took her hand. When she squeezed it, he reacted with the same excitement as a lad at Eton experiencing his first flirtation. He kissed her hand. "I must speak with Rockingham."

Her face fell.

When was he ever going to get to be alone with his bride? He strode to Rockingham. "I beg a private word," Bentley said.

"Of course. Let us go to the library."

When they reached the library, Bentley explained what he'd learned from the potential investors about New Londinium and how he was only able to read about Cook's initial exposure to the island on his first voyage. "From what I read, there's certainly not enough there to warrant significant investment."

Rockingham listened to the sketchy details of that first sighting of the island. "I tend to agree with you. There's certainly not enough there to risk one's fortune."

"It's possible Cook went back on either his second or that fatal third expedition. I don't have those journals in my possession. My guess is that Admiral Lord Hawthorne would be bound to possess all of Cook's journals."

"Brilliant!"

Bentley drew in a long breath. "I can't risk the other investors learning that I am so thoroughly investigating the matter."

"You don't want to end up like Devere."

"But since you're not a potential investor, I thought perhaps you could persuade the admiral to allow you to read those later journals. You know what kind of information I'm seeking."

Rockingham nodded. "Something to justify sinking a fortune into an obscure little pup of an island."

"Exactly."

"I'll go to Hawthorne's right now."

AFTER HER HUSBAND spoke with Lord Rockingham, he returned to Emily at the same time that Lord Rockingham left. She wondered if something her husband had said caused Lord Rockingham to leave so soon after talking to Richard. How she wished it were just the two of them. She could only barely keep her hands off this man she had married.

He led her to a small game table set up in front of the fogged-up window facing the street. They sat at the table, and he drew her hand into his once more.

"What time did you return last night?" she asked.

He shrugged. "It was after two. I never expected you to wait up for me, but it would have been . . ." His voice lowered. "Enormously satisfying to find you in my bed."

Exactly the words she longed to hear. She'd been torturing herself imagining her husband in the arms of an old flame. From his current actions, it seemed as if he sincerely missed being with her. The very notion of lying beside him in his big bed thinned her breathing. She squeezed his hand, her gaze lingering on his ruggedly handsome face. He would have shaved this morning, but his hair was so thick and dark, the dark stubble was already shadowing that face she could never grow tired of.

She took some time to form her response. He must understand his neglect of her was *not* acceptable. It most definitely was not. "If you truly desire my company, you have a most peculiar way of showing it."

"We haven't had the opportunity to get to know each other

well—though I have no doubts as to your merit in every respect. As for me, I wish you to know that I don't lie."

He stared at her with those unflinching black eyes of his. There was such sincerity in them and in his words, she felt guilty for doubting his affection.

Did he fear she was questioning his fidelity? She certainly had questioned it. "Rather than lie, then, you merely say *I am not at liberty to say*." There was mirth in her voice.

He grinned. "You do understand me."

"I hope the day will come when we completely understand one another."

"It will."

She sighed. "Will I have the pleasure of my husband's company tonight?"

"I'm planning on it." He lifted her hand and pressed it with his lips.

"What did you say to Lord Rockingham to make him hasten away so quickly?"

He shrugged. "Lord Rockingham's a very important man. I dare say his parliamentary duties beckon."

"The House of Lords meets today?" She knew very well it did. It was a source of consternation that those lords often met until very late in the night.

He did not answer for a moment. She wondered if he were considering forgoing attendance in order to be with his bride. Finally, he frowned. "Regrettably."

These separations on top of the anxiety over Devere were destroying the little bit of composure she was clinging to. It was all she could do to suppress the tears from streaming along her cheeks. She was determined not to humiliate herself.

Lords Montague and Churston stood and eyed her husband. Even before they spoke, she knew it was time for them to rush off to the Palace of Westminster. Duty was calling.

Just this once, she wished her husband would put her in front of his duties. But, then, he wouldn't be that man she had fallen in love with, the man who was accomplishing much good for the betterment of mankind.

"It's that time, old fellow," Monty said. "Care to ride with us?"

Richard's solemn gaze went from her to his fellow legislators, and he stood. "I won't be sorry to see this session come to an end." He bent to press a swift kiss to his wife's cheek. "I hope to be home with my wife tonight."

To Bentley's surprise, Rockingham was already in the White Chamber, where the lords met. He couldn't possibly have already been at Admiral Lord Hawthorne's and looked over Cook's journals in so short a time. Which must mean that Hawthorne was not in. What if Hawthorne wasn't in London? Who else could offer access to those journals? The Harley family's library was the only one in London that could rival the Bentley library. His gaze shifted across the House of Lords, where he spied Lord Oxford, head of the Harley family. At least he was in town.

Just as Bentley settled on a second-row bench next to Lord Montague, Rockingham approached him with a package. Whispering, he said, "The admiral permitted me to borrow all of Cook's journals. I promised to return them within a week."

Bentley nodded. He appreciated that Rockingham had wrapped them. It wouldn't do for any of the members of the New Londinium Committee to know he was investigating their scheme.

During some of the afternoon's boring speeches, Bentley itched to be able to read those journals, or to at least scan them for any mentions of New Londinium, but that could only be done in the privacy of his own home—which would be difficult, given that when he was home, he must devote his attentions to Emily.

Bitterness lodged in him. There was nothing he wanted more

than to be able to take his wife into his arms and thoroughly make love to her. Every minute of every day, he ached for each second in her presence, he ached for the sound of her girlish voice, he ached for a glimpse of her dimpled face, but most of all, he ached for the touch of her.

He was well aware that theirs wouldn't be a complete marriage until he could resolve the situation with the New Londinium scheme, until he was at liberty to share with his wife why he'd had to be absent ever since Devere's injury. This deception was no way to start a marriage, especially for a man who prized himself upon his honesty.

He was still sitting in the House of Lords attempting to show interest in the mundane subject of the necessity of ridding one of the government buildings of dry rot as the murky afternoon sky gave way to night.

It suddenly occurred to him that he ought to consult his man of business about stock speculation as well as the possibility of earning six percent interest. It sounded awfully high to him, especially for a business that had not yet produced any marketable commodity. Bentley himself was not knowledgeable enough to make that determination. His father had always impressed upon him the need to employ capable men in possession of knowledge a duke lacked. Bentley couldn't believe any duke in the kingdom was adept in the ways of exchanging stocks.

As soon as he could reasonably make his exit—after being assured he wasn't needed for any important votes—he engaged a hackney to take him to Tolley's house in Bloomsbury. Bentley couldn't remember the last time he'd ridden in a public conveyance. He also wasn't exactly sure where in Bloomsbury his man of business resided, but with the help of the hackney driver, they found it without too much difficulty.

Fortunately, Tolley was in, and he seemed delighted that the Duke of Bentley was honoring him with his presence. "If Your Grace would be so kind, I should be delighted to present my wife to you."

"Of course. I will be glad to meet Mrs. Tolley."

Moments later, the man's middle-aged wife descended the stairs, directing a broad smile upon Bentley. She dipped into a curtsy, then her husband presented her to the duke.

"I'm honored to finally be able to meet Your Grace," she said. "Samuel speaks of you all the time." The woman, who was slightly plump, was possessed of milky skin and dark hair that was sprinkled with gray.

"It's a pleasure to meet you, Mrs. Tolley—as it's been a pleasure to have been associated with your husband ever since I inherited, and my father before me relied on your husband. He's a fine man, and he's uncommonly knowledgeable in his profession. In fact, I've come here tonight to pick his brain."

"By the way, Your Grace," Mrs. Tolley said, "we wish to offer felicitations on your marriage."

Tolley had been involved in the marriage contracts. "Thank you."

"Please, Your Grace, come to my library," Tolley said.

Though most of these houses in Bloomsbury were more modest than those in Mayfair or St. James, Tolley's library boasted generous proportions and what looked to be a fairly decent selection of books. But the focal points here were the fireplace, where a healthy fire blazed, and a large writing table stacked with assorted ledgers.

Instead of going to the table, Mr. Tolley went to the sofa in front of the fire. "Please, Your Grace, make yourself comfortable." Both men sat on the sofa of malachite green.

"How can I be of assistance to Your Grace?" Tolley asked.

"First, I need you to understand that I'm depending upon your complete discretion. What I discuss here tonight must not be repeated to anyone. Is that understood?"

"As always, Your Grace, you can count upon my discretion."

Bentley knew he could. The man had served the Dukes of Bentley faithfully for many years, and discretion was often vital to their transactions. "As I'm sure you're aware, I'm not knowledgeable about all those things you know about," Bentley said. "I haven't had to be because I have full confidence in you. Now, however, a situation has arisen in which I need some expert advice."

Tolley's brows rose.

"A family member of mine was approached by a group of prominent men who are looking to . . . I'm not sure of the proper terminology. They're in the preliminary stages of gathering investors to start a company they hope will be a lucrative business. It's in a foreign country. To my knowledge, they haven't yet collected the money or started the business, which I believe will take more than a year to establish."

Tolley nodded. "By prominent, I assume you mean these men are mostly peers?"

"Correct."

Tolley chuckled. "Meaning no offense, Your Grace, but it's my belief investments are best done by men who do nothing else."

"Men like yourself. I agree. That's why I've come here tonight."

"Surely these men have engaged the services of a stockbroker?"

"Not yet. They say they plan to, but it struck me that they're putting the horse before the cart."

"Indeed, they are. There are too many rules and regulations concerning stocks for laymen to know what they're doing."

"Tell me this: Is it possible at this preliminary a stage to be able to promise a six percent annual return on investment?"

Tolley laughed out loud.

"I think you've answered my most vital question."

"It's actually possible to lose every penny invested—especially when a company is overseen by men who don't know what they're doing."

Exactly as Bentley thought.

For the next hour, Bentley asked questions about the procedure to launch a brand-new business endeavor. It seemed to him, based on Tolley's responses, these men who had approached Devere weren't doing anything right. Good lord, had Devere told them that?

As their conversation was winding down, Bentley's gaze went to the package Lord Rockingham had obtained from Admiral Lord Hawthorne. The journals. The sooner he read them, the sooner he might be able to finish the inquiries on behalf of Devere. Surely it wouldn't take long to scan them for mention of New Londinium.

"I beg a favor," he said to Tolley.

"Anything, Your Grace."

"Could I have use of your library tonight? It shouldn't be for long. I shall need to peruse some documents in this package before I go . . . go on."

Tolley stood. "Certainly. Take as long as you need." He started toward the door. "Just ring if you need anything. Anything at all."

IT WAS AFTER midnight, and her husband still hadn't come home in spite of telling her today that he would be with her tonight. With bitterness, she recalled him also telling her he did not lie. Was she the only person he lied to?

And why did he lie? Where was he going every night when he was supposed to be with his wife? As badly as it hurt, she was convinced he must be in love with another woman. He'd only married her because, as a Beresford, she was a suitable wife for a prominent duke.

She felt like weeping.

CHAPTER TWELVE

BY HALF PAST eleven, Bentley was finished at Tolley's house. He'd spent over an hour scanning through the rest of James Cook's journals, looking for any reference to the island of New Londinium. Not a single reference appeared after the initial entries from the first expedition.

At first, Bentley thought he must have missed such a reference. Therefore, he looked through those hundreds of pages one more time. Still, the result was the same. Captain James Cook never returned to New Londinium. He never wrote in any way about trying to locate a gold mine on the island. He never intended to go back to the diminutive island in the Atlantic.

Where did those potential investors acquire information that would encourage them to sink a fortune into so shaky an investment? It was bad enough they were risking their own money, but as he understood it, the British government was poised to contribute hefty amounts into the endeavor, money the kingdom could ill afford to lose. Especially now, when the costly war had depleted the treasury.

It wasn't until he was leaving Tolley's house that he remembered he'd come in a hackney because he'd gone off to Parliament in Monty's coach instead of his own. He stood little chance of finding a hackney in this residential neighborhood. If he walked down to High Holborn, his chances of catching one would be better.

From Tolley's house, which was just around the corner from the Duke of Bedford's Russell Square, he walked out into the misty night, heading in the direction of High Holborn. What a pity he had no coat! It was beastly cold. Thick fog shortened his vision so he couldn't see past the house next to the Tolleys'.

It was obvious this area was populated by families, families all cocooned in their beds at this hour. Nary a window he passed was lighted. No conveyances moved along these streets.

Yet the sound of footsteps on the pavement behind him echoed his own. At first, he did not give it a thought. But when the steps persisted for more than five minutes, it occurred to him that it was possible he was being followed.

To confirm his suspicions, he stopped at the next corner and tried to appear as if he were considering which way to turn. The steps behind him stopped. His chest tightened. *I am being followed.* A pity he had no weapon. He vowed to be more cautious in the future. But what to do now?

Was he being followed by a thief? Or had his follower been sent by one or more members of the New Londinium Committee? Was he being suspected of aiding Devere in his inquiries? If only Devere could have given him more guidance. Was Devere even ready to challenge the committee members?

Bentley's first instinct was to confront his follower and demand to know who'd sent him. But what if his follower was nothing more than a common thief? That seemed unlikely, given that Bentley had spent nearly three hours at Tolley's. What petty thief would wait for so long?

He turned in the direction of High Holborn and sped up his pace. The steps behind him also accelerated. Minutes later, he reached the street where he hoped to find a hackney. High Holborn was more brightly lit and accommodated more foot and vehicular traffic, which he found comforting.

Because of the fog and darkness, it was difficult to spy a hackney, but since his hearing was more reliable than his sight in this wretched fog, he thought perhaps one was clopping along near a public house half a minute's walk away. He started in that direction.

So did the footsteps behind him.

If he crossed the street, perhaps he could get a glimpse of his follower in a reflection off one of the storefront windows. He went quickly to the north side of the street. His follower stayed on the south side and continued on at the same pace as Bentley.

The ever-thickening fog, as well as the distance, made it impossible for Bentley to see his follower's reflection in the passing windows.

Soon, a slowly rolling hackney came into view some twenty-five feet from him. He rushed toward it, shouting for it to stop.

Fortunately, the driver heard him and stopped as Bentley approached. "To Grosvenor Square, my good man." Bentley spoke in a loud enough voice to assure being heard on the other side of the street.

The driver's gaze whisked over the fine clothing Bentley wore, and he smiled. "Be there in a jiffy, gov'nah."

As Bentley climbed into the coach, he glimpsed the man hanging back on the opposite side of the street, watching him. The dark-haired man, of a similar age to Bentley, did not dress as a man of means. Was he a thief? Or had he been hired to follow Bentley and report on his activities?

When the coach sped off, Bentley lifted the curtain and eyed the man standing on the south side of High Holborn, watching after the hired conveyance. At least he wasn't going to follow him now.

If the man had been hired to follow Bentley, he would be acquainted with where his quarry lived. And he would have been waiting outside the Palace of Westminster to follow Bentley when he left that building many hours earlier.

It was well past midnight when Bentley arrived home. He winced at the lateness of the hour. Once more, he had failed to keep his word to Emily, even after he had told her he would be home with his bride tonight.

And once more, he was disappointed to find his bed empty. He moved like a cat to her bedchamber. Her room was in near total darkness, save for the waning glow from the fire. Only her sweet rose scent indicated her presence, that and the soft breathing of a woman deep in sleep.

He had let her down. Again.

Was this mission for her cousin going to completely destroy their marriage?

EMILY DIDN'T KNOW who to blame for her current misery: Jeremy Bentham or her husband. As brilliant as he was, Mr. Bentham's book was as effective as laudanum for putting her to sleep each night since she had married. If his writings were more interesting, perhaps she could have kept awake until the late hour when her husband returned.

Her husband. She was beginning to doubt even the veracity of her marriage. She had not spent much over an hour in his company since the day of the ceremony that supposedly united them. As deeply as she loved him, she felt no more married to him than she did to the Prince Regent himself.

Yesterday morning she had believed Richard's sincerity when he'd vowed to be home with her that night. But once again, he'd let her down. He was proving not to be a man of his word in spite of what he'd told her about his inherent honesty.

Whenever one of the servants referred to her as *Your Grace*, she felt like an imposter. Her emotions were splintering like broken glass. When she was alone with Richard, he made her feel as if he was in love with her. But he must not be. When you loved someone, you wanted to be with that person.

What was keeping him away from her? She had learned from her sisters at precisely what time their husbands had returned from the House of Lords and learned that they—unlike Richard—had come home at a reasonable hour. So, Richard must be lying to her. The explanation she kept coming back to for his duplicity terrified her: he was seeing another woman, a woman with whom he must be in love.

It fairly broke her heart to come to such a realization. She was so torn up, every facet of her life was seen through a thick layer of gloom. Throughout her life, she had shared her hopes, joys, and disappointments with her sisters, particularly with Georgiana, who was the closest to her in age.

Now, though, she held onto her heartbreak as if it were shame. She couldn't burden Georgiana with her own marital failures, especially given that both Georgiana and Lucy were in marriages with men who adored them and wished to be with their wives more than with anyone else. Hence, Lords Montague and Churston came straight home to their wives when they left Parliament.

Not so with the Duke of Bentley.

If he would not tell Emily where he was going each night, and if she could not share her crushing suspicions with her sisters, there was just one thing to do. Tonight she would contrive to follow him. Not knowing where he was going each night was eating into her like a corrosive acid.

She had rushed here to Devere House as soon as she had dressed that morning. She did not want to see Richard. She loathed confrontations, and in her present state of anger she wished to avoid being shrewish with him.

The news about Devere contributed even more to the gloom which settled over her and her family members like a leaden blanket. He had shown no improvement over the past four-and-twenty hours.

She eyed Harriett as her cousin sat there stroking a fluffy orange cat. Harriett had been only barely short of hysteria ever since her brother had been so gravely injured. "Would you please do me the goodness of walking with me to St. George's?" Emily asked. "I dare say you and I ought to light candles for Devere."

One of the reasons Emily wanted to leave Devere House was so she wouldn't have to see Richard. She knew as soon as he awakened, he would be heading here to inquire about her cousin's progress.

She was afraid that in her present state of agitation, she would initiate a confrontation that would be embarrassing to all.

"Oh, yes! I should love to light a candle for my brother." Harriett said. "That's just what's needed right now. Allow me to get my cloak and bonnet."

A moment later, the two women were leaving Devere House just as the Duke of Bentley was entering. Their eyes met. His brightened. "Good morning, my love."

She stiffened and spoke formally. "Good morning, Your Grace." Then, trembling, she turned her back to him and descended the steps. When she reached the pavement, she was aware that he stood at the top step and watched her.

She had fed him a dose of his own negligence.

As bad as Bentley's own disappointment was, it hurt even more to know that he was responsible for destroying his wife's sweet disposition, for destroying her affection toward him, possibly even for destroying her love for him. He knew as well as he knew he resided on Grosvenor Square that his bride had been in love with him. Did she not realize how much he loved her, how besotted he was over her?

This visit to Devere House had brought him nothing but frustration. First, his wife had snubbed him, then he learned Devere showed no progress toward recovery. There were so many aspects of this inquiry he would like to run by Devere. How far had Devere gotten in his investigation? What did Devere think he'd done to disclose his suspicions about the stock scheme?

Who did he suspect of ordering his murder?

Thank God Devere hadn't been murdered. Bentley's gut clinched. Not yet, anyway.

He left Devere House to attend the House of Lords. Today he would use his own coach. Perhaps he would finally get to spend this night with his wife.

In the White Chamber while he was speaking with Lord Gray, Lord Abbott, who was Chancellor of the Exchequer, approached him. At first he made small talk about the weather, but when Lord Gray was called away, Lord Abbott said, "I am told by Fletcher that you have some interest in joining the New Londinium Committee."

"That's true."

"That's splendid. We need men like you, men of ample means and lofty titles. We're getting much closer to launch. We would be honored if you would join us tonight. My house on Cavendish Square. A group of key investors will be dining with me. All men."

Bentley felt like groaning. Though Emily was more important to him than his own life, he was being asked to choose between her and Devere's investigation. He drew a deep breath. Devere had indicated that the country, their beloved Britain, could be ruined if this stock offering proved to be as ill-conceived as he suspected.

As Bentley stood there among the drone of voices in the House of Lords, he knew he must choose between his wife and his country. No man should ever have to make such a sacrifice.

"Then I shall see you at dinner," Bentley said.

Chapter Thirteen

Like the Beresfords and Bentleys, Lord Abbott's family was one of the oldest in England. His house on Cavendish Square was easily the most impressive as well as the largest one there with its classical Doric columns flanking each window as well as the oversized doorway. The man himself had been a power broker for as long as Bentley could remember and had served as Chancellor of the Exchequer for almost a decade. Because he was twenty years older than Bentley and because he was a grandee of the Tories, the two had never been close.

Bentley was shown to the drawing room where Lords Abbott, Fletcher and Sloane were drinking Madeira. Was that all who would be here tonight? Perhaps he would be able to make it home to his wife in time to make amends for his shameful neglect of her.

He still had been unable to dispel the festering questions about the man who'd followed him last night, though he was confident it had something to do with the New Londinium project. Even though Bentley had considered confronting his stalker, he was glad he'd decided against doing so. It was best the committee members not know he was suspicious.

Was one of the men in this chamber tonight responsible for having him followed? Would his actions the past few days be construed as suspicious? Had he done anything that could provoke a threat on his life? Was he to meet the same fate as Devere—or worse?

He prayed these men would not learn of his marriage. Emily had become his Achilles heel. For himself, he was not concerned. For her, he worried. He would do anything to keep her safe.

All three men stood when he entered the opulent chamber that had been decorated in gilded furnishings and silks in a rich, deep orange. Lord Abbott walked up to him and shook his hand. "Good of you to come tonight, Your Grace. Allow me to pour you Madeira."

Bentley stuck by his side as Lord Abbott poured his wine. Then all four men sat upon the matching sofas in front of a fireplace of Carrara marble and drank their Madeira while waiting to be summoned to the dinner room.

"I cannot convey to you how happy we were to learn that Your Grace might be interested in our little endeavor," Lord Abbott said. "I will own, my initial impetus was to find a way to shore up our country's depleted treasury. And while that is still the driving goal of our committee, I now believe it's also an incredible opportunity to expand one's wealth."

Lord Fletcher nodded. "Lord Abbott has promised to issue all shareholders six percent per year for our initial investments."

Bentley hated to stir up a hornet's nest, especially after the attempted murder of Devere, but he didn't want to seem too eager to blindly follow these men with what he suspected was an ill-planned scheme. It seemed to him these men would be just as skeptical of one who could be easily duped as of one who asked a great many questions—which is what Devere must have been doing.

"I hate to ask stupid questions," Bentley began, "but how can you know at this stage that you'll be able to pay such interest? With business ventures, does one not have to be prepared to *not* make a profit at first?"

"Oh, of that you're right, Your Grace," Lord Abbott said. "What we're doing here, though, is essentially setting up our own bank, which, of course, a government cannot do. We need men of means to establish the bank. It is actually the bank which is agreeing to pay the interest to the shareholders in exchange for the capital they've contributed to finance our company—New Londinium."

Bentley nodded. "Then the money coming from the shareholders won't be used to actually set up the company for things like settling the colony, shipping to the Atlantic, labor, materials, and such? You're saying instead that our money will be used to establish a bank?"

Lord Abbott smiled. "That's right."

"It will take funds to set up the mining enterprise," Lord Fletcher said.

Bentley might be endangering his own life with the next query, but he could not sit there and act like a brainless pawn. He, for one, would not wish to associate with stupid men when one was risking large sums of money—especially when that money could bankrupt the kingdom.

It sounded to him as if these men—all men in high government positions—were attempting to perpetuate a dangerously risky hoax.

"Has the committee been—or does it plan to go—to New Londinium to gauge the potential success of this endeavor? For example, does it not need to be established that there actually is a source of gold there? Do we not need to know if the natives are hostile, or can they be befriended? Before laying out large amounts of money, we need to know if this plan is feasible."

Lord Abbott's brows lowered as his gaze flashed to Lord Fletcher, who looked like a child who'd just been caught with his thumb in the pudding. "That's a splendid idea, is it not, Lord Fletcher?" Abbott said.

It became increasingly more obvious that these men had not made any firm plans, yet they were attempting to gain large sums of money. Bentley had the oddest feeling he was being asked to be a party to a swindle of mammoth proportions.

What he knew of Devere convinced him that Devere was an intelligent man who would not have complied quietly. Bentley hoped to God he wasn't setting himself up for the same fate as Devere. "I would have thought an expeditionary force would already have been sent."

Lord Sloane shrugged. "That takes money."

"May I ask which men thus far have become founding members?" Bentley asked.

"We hope to be able to put your name at the top of our list," Lord Fletcher said. "You and your family are highly respected—and it's well-known that you're one of the wealthiest men in the kingdom."

"So true," Lord Abbott concurred. "But Fletch, His Grace needs to know who else will be on our founders' committee." He eyed Bentley. "In addition to us three in this chamber—"

Abbott's butler entered the chamber. "Dinner is ready, my lord."

"Ah, we'll continue this discussion at the table," Lord Abbott said.

The four men proceeded to the dinner room which was ablaze with the glow from a pair of huge, silver candelabra. Leaves had been removed from the table to make it smaller in order to foster congenial conversation. As the highest-ranking person there, Bentley sat next to Lord Abbott.

The tureen of clear turtle soup was passed around. "Now where were we?" Bentley asked. He was anxious to get on with the discussion. The sooner they imparted the information, the sooner he could be with Emily.

"I believe you asked about what men have made pledges to this endeavor," Lord Abbott said. "So far, all the commitments have come from Tories. Understandably, we wish to include all Englishmen in this opportunity."

"You will remember the men who met at my house?" Lord Fletcher said to Bentley.

"Oh, yes." Bentley chuckled. "I kept expecting you fellows to beg me to switch my allegiance in the House of Lords."

They all laughed.

"Each man at my house that night has agreed to be one of the founding members," Lord Fletcher said.

"And we have about ten more men who are close to making a commitment," Lord Sloane added.

Bentley's eyes narrowed. He hated his role as devil's advocate, but he could not play the role of compliant idiot. "It would seem to me a great many more members are needed. Should the number of investors not be in the hundreds?"

He had refrained from leveling the sternest criticism regarding the committee's lack of planning. How could they not have considered exploring the island before rushing off with so costly a scheme that might never come to fruition? At this point, he saw no evidence of the scheme's potential for success.

"That is, indeed, a savvy question," Lord Abbott said as the turbot was brought out, and the men began passing it around the table. "You are correct, Your Grace. We shall need hundreds of investors, but I believe our founders, which currently number around twenty, are our most important asset. We would be honored to have you as a founding member."

"Indeed," Lord Fletcher said. "With names like our illustrious Chancellor of the Exchequer and the Duke of Bentley, we are sure others will want to be part of our exciting endeavor."

"Do you plan to publish these names in the newspapers?" Bentley asked.

"We do," Abbott answered.

"And what kind of investment will our country's treasury be required to make?" Bentley asked.

The smile on Abbott's face dimmed. "That has yet to be determined."

"I'm assuming such an expenditure will have to be voted upon in Parliament?" Bentley eyed Lord Abbot.

Bentley did not miss the furtive glances Abbott and Fletcher exchanged. "We are investigating that feasibility right now," the chancellor said.

"Then we will need to cultivate support of members of Parliament." Bentley deliberately used *we* to give the impression he would be supporting their ill-planned scheme.

Lord Abbott nodded. "That's another reason why we are so delighted to welcome you to our committee. We hope you can persuade some other Whigs to join us."

Bentley felt he now understood the scheme, and from what he'd learned, he could well understand Devere's skepticism. "I believe you gentlemen have answered all my questions." He was desperate to go home and be with his wife.

FROM WITHIN THE dark cubicle inside the rented hack, Emily had watched her husband enter the finest house on Cavendish Square. She knew her husband was an extremely wealthy man, but surely such a fine home could not belong to a woman who was a courtesan, her husband's mistress. Since London was not her home, she did not know residents of the city's upper-class neighborhoods. She tapped upon the coach to attract the driver's attention. He came around and opened the door.

"I wish you to acquaint me with the name of the person who owns that fine white house." She pointed to the one her husband had entered.

"Oh, miss, I can tell ye. That house belongs to the Chancellor of the Exchequer."

"Lord Abbott?"

"Indeed, Your Grace."

Then it wasn't the house of her husband's ladybird! Relief swished over her like water dousing a fire. She knew Lord Abbott was a Tory, and she was curious to know why her husband, whose circle was comprised almost exclusively of Whigs, would be neglecting his own wife in order to spend time with a man he must oppose.

Sitting in this hackney was exceedingly boring. She'd begun late that afternoon. She'd particularly wanted to follow Richard when he left Parliament. Though she wanted nothing more than having him race home to be with her, she had instinctively known he would not be coming straight home.

Knowing that he wasn't with his ladybird offered her some solace. But still, she was offended that he did not desire to be with her. She certainly craved being with him, even though she was hurt, angry, and humiliated by his disinterest in her.

She supposed he was at Lord Abbott's to discuss governmental affairs. The night was early yet. Would he go to his mistress when he left here?

She intended to find out.

Because of the hour, she surmised the men were conducting their business over the dinner table. Which made her realize how hungry she was. *I must get my mind off my discomfort.*

As she sat there with the curtain pulled back enough to watch the entrance of Lord Abbott's fine home, she noticed another unmarked coach on the opposite side of the square from Abbott House. Its driver was poised to commence his journey, and she was certain a passenger was peering from the window inside the coach. Just like her.

Someone else was being followed. How interesting.

Almost three hours after he entered the house on Cavendish Square, her husband left. Just seeing him skip down the steps quickened her pulse. She could never grow tired of peering at him and his blatant masculinity. No man could ever favorably compare to him; on no other man except her husband could she ever bestow her heart. She was incapable of loving any man except him, and it was sheer torture to gaze upon him and know she did not hold his love.

As she had previously instructed, her driver began to follow the ducal coach at a discreet distance.

Since the driver would be diligent about keeping his eye on

the Bentley coach, her gaze moved to that other unmarked coach that had been lingering in Cavendish Square. To her astonishment, it also began to move. Perhaps she'd been wrong about it following someone. There surely was no reason anyone else would be interested in where her husband was going.

Knowing how tedious it was to wait for hours when following one's quarry, she supposed the other man—for she thought the glimpse she'd seen was of a man—must have given up on waiting.

Moments later, her husband disembarked from his coach at Devere House. It saddened her to think Richard might have come there in the hopes of seeing her.

Oddly, he was carrying the same package he'd been carrying earlier that day. At the time, she had assumed it was a gift for his ladybird. Now she knew she'd been wrong. Had she also been wrong about him having a ladybird? What was in that package? Why was her husband toting it about the Capital?

She felt guilty for not already being at her cousin's house. Waiting carriages in front belonged to the Rockinghams, the Montagues, and the Churstons.

Was her husband hoping to see her there? Is that why he'd come here straight from Lord Abbott's? She still could not dispel the thought that he'd been hiding something from her. But, if she had been wrong about him being in love with another woman, what could it be?

Her hackney rolled to a stop three houses away from Devere House. She kept peering from the window. That other unmarked coach had also turned onto Curzon Street, and it stopped opposite her. She watched to see if its occupant was getting out, but he remained seated inside the vehicle.

Just like her.

It now became abundantly clear to her that man was following her husband.

But why?

Such knowledge confirmed her suspicions. Richard was involved with something or someone he was hiding from her. She prayed it wasn't another woman.

So she would be waiting once again. Time, under these circumstances, seemed to drag by as slowly as growing hair.

She had no way of knowing how long Richard was at Devere's house, but it was not very long. When he emerged, he was no longer carrying that package. She was more consumed with curiosity than ever to learn its contents.

She regretted how rude she'd been to him that morning. He had deserved it, but her hostility would make it more difficult for them to reconcile.

At the thought he might be coming to be with her, her heartbeat drummed madly. The hackney driver began to follow Richard. She prayed he'd be coming to her. Coming home.

When his coach rounded the corner onto Grosvenor Square, she could have wept with joy. He was coming home to her tonight!

It was important to her that she handsomely pay the hackney driver for her monopoly on his time these past several hours—and do so quickly—then she would hasten into their house.

As she was gathering coins from her reticule, a coach passed by. She glanced out the window and saw it was the same one that had apparently been following her husband. It came to a stop around the corner from one of the entrances to the square. It was obvious to her the driver was watching Bentley House.

Why would someone be following her husband?

If Richard did not know he was being followed, he needed to know. And she was going to demand an explanation.

She paid the driver and rushed up the steps to Bentley House. It was still difficult to think of it as her house—just as difficult as it was to think herself a married woman when she was still a maiden.

When she entered the house, Richard was almost at the top of the stairway, and he turned to see her. A smile brightened that face she adored, and he reversed himself to come to her. "I'm so happy to make it home while my wife is still awake."

She was, too. But she was not yet ready to let him know that. "I suggest we go to your library. We need to talk."

The smile on his face faded. "*Our* library."

She was determined to present a stern countenance. Before he reached the ground floor, she pivoted and strode to the library, going straight to the crimson velvet sofa in front of the fire. He came to sit close to her.

"And what, my beautiful wife, do we need to discuss?"

It was all she could do not to drape herself around him. She craved his every touch. She cherished the sound of his masculine voice. She wanted nothing more than to be with him. But she needed to remain solemn, to force him to be honest with her about what he'd been doing these past several nights.

She prayed he hadn't been with his lover.

"I must know where you've been going every night. I want to trust you. I want to believe that you have always been honest with me, but it's difficult, given your prolonged absences." She drew a breath. "I've feared you're in love with another woman."

He broke out laughing.

She glared.

"Forgive me, my love," he said. "I am truly delighted that you care enough about me to worry there's another woman. I assure you, there's not. You are the only woman I've ever loved."

Tears gathered in her eyes. "I have a confession."

His face blanched.

Did he think she was going to confess she loved another man? She hurried to reassure him. "I followed you tonight."

His silence filled the chamber like a creeping fog. Her eyes locked with his black ones. Neither spoke for a moment.

"I was happy to learn you were not at a woman's house, but as your wife, I believe I am owed an explanation as to why you preferred dining with Lord Abbott instead of with your own bride."

He nodded thoughtfully but still said nothing.

"I also saw you carrying a package into Devere's, and I wish for you to tell me what was in it."

Still, he said nothing. Had she destroyed his affection by not trusting him and by following him? Did he consider her a shrew? This was a wretched way to begin a marriage.

"There's more," she added.

"Wonderful," he said sarcastically.

"Someone else was following you all night."

He cursed under his breath. Then, his expression softened, and he took her hand. "You are owed an explanation. I have been intentionally evasive because I gave my word to Devere that I would not tell you or anyone about the investigation he charged me with on our wedding night." He sighed. "But now I must tell you. For your own safety."

Her eyes rounded. What in the world could he be talking about? "Investigation?"

"Allow me to explain." He proceeded to tell her that Devere believed the theft was engineered to cover up an attempt on his life, and he explained what he had managed to learn about the New Londinium scheme. "The fact that I'm being followed may mean that one or more of those men could believe my inquiries threaten them."

Her insides crashed. She would accept a mistress over a dead husband, though both prospects sickened her—especially the contemplation of him being murdered.

"Then you could meet the same fate as my poor cousin!" The tears that had been threatening trickled now.

He brushed them away with the pad of his thumb then drew her into his arms and held her close. "I'll be careful. But, more importantly, you must be careful not to mention this to anyone. We still do not know precisely who ordered your cousin's murder."

She winced. "Don't say that word! I can't bear to think of Devere being killed." She pulled back and peered into her husband's eyes. "He must recover." More tears flowed.

"Lady Devere told me tonight she thought he was improving."

"And I couldn't bear it if . . ." She sniffed. "Something happened to you."

His head lowered, and he claimed her lips hungrily. When she felt the warmth of his tongue against hers, something low in her torso began to throb. She kissed him passionately.

"Will you come to my bed?" he asked, his voice husky.

CHAPTER FOURTEEN

FINALLY! THE WAY Emily's body reacted to this man, she would have permitted him to strip her bare and make love to her right here in the library. Her breasts felt heavy and needy for his touch. A throbbing deep down demanded to be addressed, and she knew Richard would know how to penetrate that special place. It was as if she could not get close enough to him.

Her entire body trembling, she nodded.

Her husband groaned as he stood and offered his hand. They climbed the stairs together. To her surprise, he walked past the duchess's chamber. Was she not going to dress in her lovely soft linen and lace night shift?

At this point, she was past questioning, past words. She craved this physical union with her husband as if her existence depended on it.

In his warm bedchamber, the oil lamp was not lighted. The room's only light came from the nearby fire. He stood before the fire with her, gathering her into his arms as his lips traced whisper-soft kisses on her face, beneath her ear, and along the length of her neck. Then, lower still.

Her passion-fogged brain recalled their last time here, on their wedding night, when they were interrupted by Devere's tragedy. The very memory of her husband taking her nipple into his mouth aroused her. She thought he was just about to repeat the action, but he cursed something unintelligible. "Will you allow me to remove the dress and your bloody stays?" he murmured.

She started to say, "Oh, yes, please!" but she did not want to diminish his respect for her by too closely mimicking a doxy. She must try to behave as a lady—even though, at this moment, she felt far more like a tart than a lady.

A month ago, she would have been mortified to be seen unclothed by a man. Now, the notion of freeing herself from her clothing, of feeling Richard's hands gliding over her bare flesh, excited her. Her sultry eyes met his, and she nodded.

He cradled her face within his hands and spoke softly. "I know you're a lady. I know you're innocent. But never, ever be embarrassed or shamed by what occurs in our marriage bed."

It was as if her husband had been reading her mind! It was then that from somewhere within her desire-steeped brain she recalled reading a line in one of her father's books of personal correspondence from some British public servant writing about why he never took a mistress. *A man wants his wife to be a lady in the drawing room and a trollop in the bedchamber.*

Since it was commonplace for men of their class to marry for pedigree and take a mistress for pleasure, she thought perhaps Richard would never take a mistress if she made him happy in the bedchamber.

She nodded solemnly and spoke in a breathless whisper. "I want you to teach me how to satisfy you in every way."

He groaned and began to tug at her dress. After it pooled on the floor, he unlaced her stays and freed her of them. Her breasts sprang free. She stepped out of her drawers.

His face lowered, and he drew a nipple into the warmth of his mouth and suckled. It was as if a molten heat spread from there along the length of her torso to settle low in that throbbing place. Her lower body began to unconsciously pulse against him, and her breathing uncontrollably sputtered.

He switched to her other breast as his hand lowered and

found the moist core of her. A finger slid into that slickened place, and she let out a little cry.

"Are you all right?" he asked, concern in his husky voice. "Do you want me to stop?"

With a shake of her head, her quivering hand guided him back to whatever it was he was doing to her that caused her to cry out with pleasure. Her own boldness embarrassed her, but she forced herself to remember his words. Anything a husband and wife did could not be lewd. Probably because the chamber was in darkness, she was not embarrassed over her nakedness.

The words of their wedding ceremony—*I give thee my body*—repeated through her mind like the peel of church bells. She and her beloved husband were to be as one.

He resumed that magical rhythm as her pulsing into his movement became ever more urgent.

"It's time, my love," he said in a gentle voice, backing her toward the bed.

As her husband tugged at his boots, she glided into the turned-down bed. When he tossed off his shirt, light from the fire cast a golden glow over his bare skin. Her gaze trailed along the sprinkling of dark hair centered on his broad chest. As he went to lower his breeches, she thought of politely turning away, but her daring curiosity won out.

She greedily watched as his bottoms came off and his manhood jutted out rather like a cannon. Her first thought was that something was the matter with him. None of the statues of nude men she'd seen looked anything like that huge organ.

Her breathing became even more ragged as she eyed that instrument of his, his instrument of her pleasure.

He came to lie next to her, the mattress sagging beneath his heft as he propped himself up on his side facing her. She flowed into his arms and parted her legs as she hitched a thigh over his. The head of his member brushed into her. *There.*

She was powerless to control the deep breaths that threatened to overtake her. Their lips came together for a long, scorching kiss. She likened it to igniting the fuse of a powder keg. At any moment, she would combust.

He rolled her onto her back and positioned himself between her parted thighs before lowering his head for a gentle, wet kiss as his finger slipped into her again. She pulsed against his movement. Then a second finger came in, and she rocked into his motion, panting, swirling, dripping with essence.

Now, he, too, was losing control. Gripping her tightly, his breathing was that of a man about to collapse after expending strenuous labor. He replaced his hand with that huge protrusion. He went very slow at first. "Stop me if I hurt you," he said in a breathless voice, tenderly brushing moist hair from her brow.

There was pain when he nudged her barrier, but she did not want him to stop, not when the euphoria of this blending was consuming her, taking her to a mystical place she'd never been.

She was incapable of rational thought. She kept recalling the words of their wedding ceremony and found herself believing she and Richard were merging into one, like cream into tea.

Just after the painful part, wave after wave of some indefinable pleasure kept crashing over her, seizing her, convulsing her, leaving her gasping and clutching her husband's back.

He, too, felt it. His body pulsed into her with frenzied need. "My God, I love you!" he cried out.

Soon, he collapsed beside her, a fine sheen of pure, manly sweat coating that beloved body of his.

Side by side, they lay. Their heavy breathing eventually eased back to normalcy.

Now, she finally felt as if she truly belonged to him.

WHEN HE'D FALLEN in love with Emily, he'd been attracted to her wholesome beauty and extraordinary dimples. He'd been impressed with how closely her ideas matched his own and how intelligent she was for her tender years. And though he'd desired her as a man desires a woman, he had never allowed himself to dream she would ever welcome physical intimacy so eagerly.

He could not have been more pleased over her reaction to his lovemaking. For himself, no woman had ever given him pleasure that could ever equal what he'd just experienced with his wife. Marriage to her was going to bring him immeasurable joy. No man could ever stray who possessed a wife as passionate as his Emily.

He truly had the perfect wife. In every way.

Once their breathlessness quelled, he drew her close. There was no greater contentment than lying in his bed with his wife beside him.

THE FOLLOWING MORNING, he awakened before her, attempted to dress himself, then told his man to have their breakfast brought to his bedchamber. Next, he summoned her maid and asked that she gather her mistress's clothing for today. It would be his pleasure, not Emily's maid's, to assist his beautiful wife in dressing this morning.

He personally drew open the heavy velvet draperies to flood his bedchamber with morning sunshine. Then he watched as Emily came awake. "Good morning, my love," he said.

She pulled the sheets about her bare body and sat up, smiling at him. "I am finally, really and truly your wife." A little giggle emanated from her.

God, but he loved this woman.

He gathered the dress and fresh stockings and drawers the maid had delivered and moved toward the bed. "I plan to assist my wife in dressing this morning."

He had picked up the stays and slippers from where they had been discarded on the floor the previous night.

"It's easier for me to do things by candlelight than in the light of day," she said shyly. "I'm uncomfortable being without clothing in daylight. In front of a man."

"That man is your husband." He chuckled. "I assure you, I love every inch of you."

He had fully intended to assist her in dressing, but now that he was this close to her naked body, he had other ideas. He tossed the clothing on the bed and then went to sit beside her for a lingering, passionate kiss.

He could not have prayed for a more enthusiastic response.

Her breath hitched, and she began to squirm and pant. She made not the slightest protest when he lowered the sheet to take a breast into his mouth. He gently backed her to a reclining position and lowered the sheet even more so he could give attention to her lower body as he eased down beside her, his hand finding her dripping core.

To his delight, she began fumbling with the flap of his breeches, and soon his fully aroused cock jutted out.

She wanted him as much as he wanted her.

He could not wait. Forget that he still wore boots, still wore a shirt with a stiff cravat. He widened her thighs, placed himself between them, and with frantic movements buried himself within her, pumping and driving until he called out her name and collapsed beside her, spent, breathless, and glistening with perspiration.

She clung to him like wet leaves as he peered down into her lovely face. Dark lashes lay on her cheeks, and a soft smile played at her lips. She was a portrait of contentment. He drew her even closer and brushed gentle kisses onto the crown of her head. What had he ever done to deserve such happiness?

"My darling duke, I believe you're making a harlot of me."

"Is not your ardor only for your husband?"

"Only for you, my dearest."

"Then you're no harlot. You're the perfect wife, and I'm the most fortunate man in the three kingdoms." He lifted her chin and kissed her sweetly on the mouth.

"Our breakfast will be here any moment." He sighed and got up. "I'd best fasten my breeches."

She giggled.

As soon as he made himself somewhat presentable, a knock sounded at his chamber door. He took the tray of breakfast offerings and asked the footman who delivered it to close the door.

"Now, allow me to help my duchess with her clothing."

Within a few minutes, she, too, was fully clothed, and they were eating at the settee near the fire, their tray on the tea table in front of the settee.

"Don't you feel better now that you've been truthful with me about those absences and your inquiries?" she asked.

"It is a relief, but I feel wretched that I've not kept my word to Devere."

"Don't. I will certainly never tell a soul about his suspicions, and now I'll be able to help you with our inquiries."

"Our?"

"Was it not agreed that we would share everything? I am your helpmate. You said you found me intelligent. Do you not think our two heads will be better than one?"

"I refuse to share the danger."

"Don't worry about me. Surely those men would not harm a woman. They are gentlemen, after all."

"What was done to your cousin is not the work of a gentleman."

She shrugged. "There is that, but I am determined to assist you in your inquiries."

He did not speak for a moment. "If I recall our wedding ceremony, you vowed to obey your husband."

She glared.

"I won't have you jeopardizing your life," he said, his voice stern. "It's my belief one of these men is a murderer."

Her lashes lowered, his wife said not a word.

"I promise not to be a dominating ogre of a husband, but this once—and only because I love you—will I put my foot down and demand that you stay out of this affair."

She remained completely silent, glaring at him. She was not going to be a compliant wife. He'd married a determined, stubborn, confident woman. Those attributes that had won his heart now added to his worries.

He could not help but to worry about her. If anything happened to Emily . . . it was too painful to contemplate. Now that they were truly married, he loved her even more than he ever thought possible. Without her, he wouldn't want to live.

Protecting his wife was more important even than discovering the identity of the man responsible for the attack upon Devere. He could not allow her to get in harm's way.

Her narrowed gaze shifted to the table where he had set the breakfast things. "I do believe I will help myself to breakfast." She busied herself with her breakfast plate before she continued. "We need to discuss the man who's been following you. Was yesterday the first time you know you were being followed?" she asked.

He did not answer for a moment. "The previous night, when I went to my man of business in Bloomsbury, I was followed on foot."

She clutched at her chest. "Thank God you weren't harmed!"

"I don't think I'm in danger at present."

"Why do you think you're being followed?"

"I think they—or he, or whoever it is who ordered the attack on Devere—wants to be assured that I'm not doing anything to thwart their scheme."

"But you may be! And then what? Will they try to kill you, too?"

"The only thing they could possibly know is that I may have discussed the potential investment with my stockbroker. I hardly think that qualifies as a threat to them."

She bit at her lower lip. "If only we knew what Devere had

done to displease them—or him."

He nodded.

Her eyes widened, a look of fear on her beautiful face. "Speaking of Devere, please don't visit him as long as you're being followed. They mustn't find out you're connected to him. It's too dangerous."

"Good suggestion, but I need to speak to him as soon as he's able."

"And you shall. I will press upon my sisters to notify me as soon as our cousin's able to communicate."

Did that mean she fully intended to foist herself into his investigation? He didn't need the further aggravation of worrying about his wife. Vexing woman!

SHE WAS INCAPABLE of giving him her word that she would stay out of his investigation. With or without his approval, she intended to assist him on his inquiries. What harm could come to her? It wasn't as if she would be telling anyone of their suspicions. She'd given her word that she would not acknowledge to anyone that threat to her cousin's life. She would never reveal that she knew anything about the New Londinium project.

Her chest tightened when she thought that her own husband's life could be in jeopardy. She had proven yesterday that she was capable of following him without him detecting it. Now her mission was to see that no harm came to her husband.

But how was she going to do that? She wasn't as helpless as she might look. Her father, who was exceedingly fond of his daughters, had seen to it that they knew how to use muskets and pistols. She had full confidence in her own abilities, abilities that just might outwit the evil forces at play here.

The very thought of someone trying to kill her husband was all the motivation she needed. There was nothing she wouldn't do to prevent harm coming to Richard. No woman could love her husband more than she loved hers.

A kernel of a plan began to develop . . .

Chapter Fifteen

THE SESSION AT the House of Lords was finished earlier than usual on this day. Bentley would be able to swing by White's for a while and still be home with his wife tonight. The memory of his wife's passion filled him with a bubbling sense of contentment.

As he'd looked around the White Chamber at other lords, he found himself wondering if any of these men loved their wives as much as he loved Emily. His wife had to be superior to all their wives in every way. Of that he was certain. He was also certain of how honored he was to have won her affection. No man's happiness could exceed his.

His life would be total perfection were it not for this wretched situation Devere had gotten him into. Poor Devere. Of course Bentley was obliged to continue where Devere had left off—if only he knew precisely what Devere had discovered. Even were Bentley not now a part of Devere's family, he would have felt obligated to pursue Devere's inquiries in order to protect his country's treasury.

If the New Londinium project was as ill-conceived and doomed to failure as Bentley feared, it had the potential to bankrupt their kingdom. He would never have been able to live with himself if he failed his country. Without hesitation, he had picked up Devere's gauntlet and continued the fellow's inquiries.

Now that he knew enough of the New Londinium scheme to fairly reliably predict its failure, there were two considerations now facing him. First, he must learn the identity of the person or persons responsible for injuring Devere. That person needed to be prosecuted. Secondly, and just as difficult as the first consideration, was deciding how to deal with the flaws of the New Londinium scheme. Someone needed to question the defects in the proposed project, but he did not especially want to be that person. He had no desire to end up like Devere. Especially now that he was married.

When it occurred to him that at this very moment Emily could be carrying their child—conceived last night, or this morning—a nearly levitating sense of joy swept over him. He'd sat there in the ancient room where the House of Lords were seated and wondered if one day his son—their son—would carry on. At the notion, a pride as great as he'd felt on his wedding day surged through him.

At White's he would launch subtle inquiries as to the financial solvency of the men already committed to the New Londinium scheme. It seemed to him that the man—or possibly men—who wanted to silence Devere desperately needed the money being raised by the New Londinium investors. So, Bentley must find out which man or men were in such desperate need.

When he arrived at White's, he nodded to a group of fellows who had been at Oxford with him. One of them beckoned him over. He was only too happy to oblige.

"Not used to seeing an old Whig like yourself at White's," Jonathan Whitby said.

Bentley shrugged. "One must broaden one's horizons." He eyed Whitby and another acquaintance from Oxford, Viscount Ogilvy. "Besides, it's good to reacquaint myself with old friends."

"Any truth to the rumor you plan to marry that last Beresford sister, who just happens to be the prettiest?" Lord Ogilvy asked.

Bentley's gut plummeted. It hadn't occurred to him that Emily would be dragged into the conversation, that others knew of his plans to marry her. "I would be most the fortunate man in the kingdom to win the affections of the lovely Miss Emily Beresford." Perhaps he had said more than he should have, but he could never deny his attraction to her.

"If I weren't already married, I'd be joining the lady's admirers," Lord Ogilvy said, "not that I'd stand much of a chance competing against a duke."

"Well, good luck to you," Whitby said to Bentley. "I saw you eating with Lords Fletcher and Sloane here recently. One must hope you're considering joining the Tories."

Bentley shrugged again. "Anything's possible. I wasn't that well acquainted with Sloane or Fletcher. I do hope they're agreeable men."

"Oh, yes," Lord Ogilvy said. "Not that one can ever have a real conversation with Sloane. He's so horse mad. All he can talk about are his stables and race meetings."

"Ah," Whitby added, "the race meetings have not been kind to Lord Sloane as of late. He's so proud of his horses, he thinks they'll win every race they enter and consequently wagers hefty sums on his own brood."

Lord Ogilvy nodded. "I hear he recently lost a packet at Newmarket."

This was exactly the type of information Bentley was seeking. Was Sloane so desperate for money that he'd be a party to a giant swindle? "If his horses are losing, one would think that might also negatively impact his stud enterprise," Bentley said.

Whitby shrugged. "The Sloane stables still have a solid reputation."

"Yes," Lord Ogilvy concurred, "that reputation has been earned over many decades and can take a while to decline."

"I hope his losses have not impacted the way he lives. He seems to be a nice fellow." Bentley laughed. "For a Tory." Bentley wondered how much of his own money Sloane was putting into New Londinium. That was one of the areas Bentley needed to further explore. How much was each man investing?

As one of the wealthiest men in the kingdom, Bentley knew he would be expected to invest heavily. Had Devere committed to investing his money?

Bentley had hoped Emily would have sent word that afternoon that Devere was awake, alert, and eager to talk to him. Unfortunately, no such announcement had been forthcoming, and Bentley still felt as if he were staggering in the dark through a maze.

Whitby eyed him. "You've no doubt heard about Devere?"

It took Bentley a moment to form his response. "Terrible. Hard to believe that happened in his own house."

"My servants have been sternly warned that our doors are to be locked at all times," Lord Ogilvy added. "Terrifying what happened to Devere. And he's a fine man. For a Whig."

They forced chuckles.

Bentley felt guilty for not further praising Devere—whom he genuinely admired—but he needed to give the illusion he was not close at all to Devere. Or to Emily. Devil take it!

"Won't you join us for dinner?" Whitby asked Bentley, standing so they could move into the dining room.

"As much as I would enjoy it, I have a previous engagement." Bentley would finally dine with his wife tonight.

SINCE HER SISTERS and her cousin Harriett were all married to peers, Emily could not borrow their carriages for her clandestine activities because they all bore their family crests. For her purposes, an unmarked coach was necessary, and she knew a hackney cab would be too easily identifiable. Therefore, when she went to Devere House to inquire about her injured cousin's progress—no change reported—she begged a private word with her brother.

Even though he hailed from an illustrious family, James, like his father before him, refused to display the Beresford crest upon his coach because he was not a title holder.

"You're the best of brothers," Emily said to him. "And cousin, too. I know how much you would prefer to be back at Tilford, but your concern for Devere has kept you in London."

"I will not return to Tilford until Devere is fully recovered and is his old self," James said.

"Which we know will happen, hopefully soon."

"Indeed."

"I have a favor to ask of you."

James's brows hiked.

"Please lend me your coach. Don't ask why, but I'm in need of an unmarked coach."

"Most women who'd just married a duke would be flaunting it all over the Capital. Why are you and Bentley not announcing your nuptials yet?"

She did not wish to explain, could not explain. "We will. Soon."

He looked at her as if he could see through her subterfuge. "I don't suppose you're going to tell me why you have need for an unmarked carriage."

"Right. I'm not ready to tell you just yet."

He threw his hands up and smiled. It was rather like facing her late Papa, her brother so resembled their father when he was a young man. "Go ahead. Make use of my coach."

She threw her arms around him. "Thank you so. See why you're my favorite brother?"

"I'm your only brother."

"There is that." She raced off to summon her brother's coach. She was happy their old family coachman had come to London. All the Beresfords trusted him completely with their safety. On several occasions, he had thwarted highwaymen because he was always aware of his surroundings and was an excellent marksman. She explained to the coachman that she would need him to make sure his musket was packed and ready.

Her chief purpose in following her husband was to protect him from meeting the same fate that had almost killed her cousin.

Three hours after she'd been sitting in her brother's coach in front of the Palace of Westminster, she spied her husband leaving the building where the House of Lords convened. He went straight to his ducal coach. She told her coachman to follow the duke's carriage.

Just after her husband rounded the corner onto St. James, she recognized the famed bow window of White's. His coach stopped, and he went to that bastion of Tory gentlemen. She knew he typically favored gathering at Brooks's but must be coming here in connection with his inquiries on behalf of her cousin.

She conveyed to the coachmen that he must circle the block of buildings, and when he returned, he would need to park at a discreet distance from White's entrance.

Hopefully, her husband wouldn't be here long. She did not have the patient temperament for this type of clandestine surveillance. In fact, nothing could compete with it for sheer boringness. But as boring as it was, she would not allow anything to divert her attention. She fancied that her husband's life depended upon her. When Richard walked out that front door of White's, she intended to follow him. She must help to keep him safe.

The memory of their intimacy last night—and this morning—caused a fluttering in the vicinity of her heart, the heart she had so lovingly bestowed on her husband. She had never in her life felt unloved, but the love she received from Richard and the love she felt for him were altogether different from and of far more intensity than any love she had ever experienced. Would she always feel so consumed by this overwhelming love of theirs, or did long-married couples become accustomed to those powerful emotions?

Afternoon slowly turned to night, and she feared Richard would be inside White's for many hours. Shortly after darkness blackened the sky, though, he came skipping down the steps, heading for his waiting coach. She wondered where he would be going next.

When she saw that his coach was headed toward Grosvenor Square, she allowed herself to hope he was coming home, that they would be together again tonight. When his coach actually turned onto the square, she told her brother's coachman to take her to the alley behind the ducal residence. Richard needn't know she had been following him.

Moments after being left at the rear door to her house, she flew toward the home's entry and into her husband's arms. "Please tell me we're to dine together tonight," she said breathlessly.

He held her at arm's length, cupping her shoulders while he peered lovingly at her. "My wife and I *will* dine together tonight."

It was more than she had hoped for, yet she had instructed the housekeeper to see that Cook had their dinner prepared for tonight. She told the nearby footman to inform Cook the Bentleys were in for dinner and that they'd be waiting in the library.

In the library, Richard poured them Madeira, and they sat sipping it in front of the fire.

"Since I didn't hear otherwise," he said, "I assume there's been no change in Devere's condition?"

She nodded solemnly. "No change." Her sisters would have notified her had there been, and she'd seen no note in the hall.

"Any news to report regarding your . . . inquiries?" she asked.

He told her he'd gone to White's. "It occurred to me that whoever wanted to kill Devere must be desperate for the money being collected for the New Londinium scheme, so I needed to find out if any of the men who've thus far committed might have suffered any financial setbacks."

"And?"

"One of them may have. That's not to say the others are exonerated, but thus far I've learned that Lord Sloane lost heavily at the Newmarket race meetings."

"That is promising. Not for Lord Sloane, though. When you first met with Lords Fletcher and Sloane, did Lord Sloane seem eager to have you as an investor in their scheme?"

He thought about it for a moment. "No more so than Lord Fletcher."

"And Lord Abbott wasn't there that first night, was he?"

"No."

"How eager did he seem when you first talked to him about it?"

"He was definitely pleased. As much as for the money they want me to invest, I believe they were just as enthusiastic about using my name to recruit other investors."

She lowered her voice and traced slow circles on his muscled thigh. "I know from personal experience how well sought after dukes are."

He leaned down to brush his lips across hers. "I never took you for a title seeker."

"You're right. Titles don't impress me. It was you—your ideas, your empathy, and . . . your physical attributes that attracted me. I would have fallen in love with you had you no title."

He kissed her again, this one slow and lingering.

Then the footman rapped at the door. The youthful servant opened it and announced, "Dinner is served Your Graces."

While they ate, she decided she would launch some sleuthing of her own. While she would never lie to Richard, she hoped to be successful at hiding her investigation from her husband. The darling man worried too much about her. She would be fine. After all, only a handful of family members knew she was the Duchess of Bentley. No one would suspect her of knowing about the Duke of Bentley's involvement in the New Londinium scheme.

CHAPTER SIXTEEN

BEFORE HE WENT to the House of Lords the following day, Bentley swung by Lord Rockingham's house. He was shown to the library, where Rockingham was seated at a large writing table, perusing stacks of pending legislation. A cat was attempting to leap onto his lap, but Rockingham kept batting him—or was it a her?—back. He looked up at Bentley. "Missed you at Devere House this morning."

The gray cat settled for climbing atop Rockingham's table and plopping itself on a second stack of parliamentary bills.

"Any progress to report about Devere?" Bentley asked.

"Actually, the surgeon is optimistic. He says the bleeding has stopped, and Devere's breathing is good. According to the surgeon, Devere's body just needs to rest to fight through the severe injury. The surgeon advocates keeping him sedated with the laudanum while he recovers."

"And Lady Devere is agreeable to all of this?"

"She has to put her trust in the surgeon. Poor woman. She's half mad with worry. Won't leave his side."

Bentley found himself wondering how Emily would react if he had been so severely wounded. As tender-hearted as she was, he suspected she'd be just as distraught as Lady Devere. "I won't be coming to Devere House anymore," Bentley said.

Lord Rockingham set down his papers and eyed his visitor

with concern. "Why?"

"I'm being followed. I can't risk allowing my followers to know that I'm close to the man they tried to kill." Bentley had no doubt the one following him had to have been involved with the theft and murder attempt at Devere House.

Lord Rockingham winced. "Then it's best you stay away from Devere House. Can't have you ending up like Devere. I don't suppose you've been able to identify the follower? Or, better yet, the man responsible for wanting Devere dead?"

Bentley shook his head. "I've seen enough of the follower to know he's likely just a hired hand. He's definitely not one of the men associated with the New Londinium plan. I've still not identified the man responsible for ordering Devere's murder. I thought perhaps that person was desperate for money and wanted to destroy anyone who was a threat to their shaky scheme."

"That sounds plausible. Any leads?"

"Thus far, one. I learned—from hearsay reported at White's, not based on solid fact—that Lord Sloane has lost a considerable amount on wagering at Newmarket."

Rockingham rolled his eyes with disgust. "Would that the man cared as much about the House of Lords as he did about his damned horses."

"He does seem to be single-mindedly obsessive over the beasts."

"His losses could give him a motive to silence Devere. I suppose you have found that Sloane is passionate about the New Londinium plan?"

"I wouldn't say passionate. He favors the investment but hasn't been overly persuasive to me."

"Hmmm. Which of the men you're dealing with would you say is the most persuasive?" Rockingham asked.

"They're all advocates, to be sure, but none passionately. I suppose Lord Abbott's the one who seems the most eager to secure my backing. Do you know if he's in financial need?"

Rockingham shrugged. "Can't say that I do." He pursed his lips in contemplation. "I do have something to share about one of the men, something negative."

"Which one?"

"Fletcher. I don't like to spread gossip, whether it's fact or repeating rumor, but under these circumstances, I feel I must. At least to you."

"I know how close you and Devere are. Quite naturally, you'll do anything in your power to find the man responsible for his injuries. So what do you know about Fletcher?"

"I don't know anything about his financial situation, but I believe I'm one of the few men in England who know what kind of cruelty he's capable of."

Bentley's eyes narrowed. "Cruelty?"

"Yes. He was gone from Eton by the time Devere and I entered, but I learned of something that occurred while he was a student there. My friend, Hugh Woolley, shared a frightening tale about Fletcher. It seems Fletcher nearly killed Woolley's older brother, who had attended Eton with Fletcher."

"Good lord! What happened?" Bentley asked.

"According to Woolley, Fletcher was out of charity with his brother and dared the Woolley lad to climb from their upper-floor window one night and shimmy down a nearby tree. It was a freezing, snowy night, and the ground was blanketed with snow. As soon as Woolley descended from the open window, Fletcher slammed it shut and locked it. The poor Woolley boy was dressed only in a night shirt. He tried to get back in his chamber, but Fletcher denied him. The lad nearly froze to death. He finally resorted to screaming out for help. He was saved, then was punished, but he never disclosed that it was Fletcher who had locked him out."

"Noble fellow. Pity Fletcher never even received a reprimand."

Rockingham nodded. "Unfair, to be sure."

"Your story does reveal a serious cruel streak in one of the

New Londinium committee members." Bentley sighed. "Of course, lads' consciences aren't fully formed, are they? I'm sure many of us did things while at Eton that shame us now."

"That's true."

Another cat—this one orange—came prancing into the chamber and also leapt on top of Rockingham's writing table, moving papers around with its paw while Rockingham cringed.

"I didn't know you were such a cat lover," Bentley said.

Rockingham slowly shook his head. "I'm not."

"Let me guess. It's your bride."

Lord Rockingham nodded. "She dotes on all creatures, and with our marriage, I seem to have inherited the lot of them, much to my consternation."

Bentley chuckled, then stood. "It would make my inquiries much easier if I were able to communicate with Devere. Please let me know as soon as he awakens."

FOR A SECOND night in a row, Emily was to have her husband home. Last night had been perfect. He'd shared with her what he'd learned from his inquiries, and after dinner they'd sipped port in front of the fire in his bedchamber. That cozy intimacy led to incredibly satisfying love making. Three different times, Richard had lifted her to frenzied, soaring heights of ecstasy. It was well past midnight when they'd finally collapsed into sleep, their bare bodies entwined with one another.

Tonight they had enjoyed dining together, and he'd told her about Lord Rockingham's tale of Lord Fletcher's sadistic nature with the elder Woolley brother. "That sounds like the kind of man who would maliciously order the execution of my sweet cousin," she said. "Lord Fletcher must be the evil man responsible for Devere's injuries."

Her husband shrugged. "He is a strong suspect, but we cannot dismiss Lord Sloane, either. Money—or the lack of it—is a strong motivator for evil-doings."

She frowned. "You're right. We have two perfectly plausible suspects in the attempt on poor Devere's life. I suppose it's even possible they planned Devere's murder together."

"It's possible, but I think it's more likely to be on the order of a single man. I just wish I knew which one."

"I suppose it's even conceivable that another of the investors could be in worse financial straits than Lord Sloane."

"True. I feel so impotent. Even after several days, I'm no closer to identifying the potential killer than I was that first night."

"But you've at least learned about New Londinium. I dare say you know more about it than any of the investors do."

His dark eyes bored into hers. "Except for the Evil One. I believe he knows the plan will never come to fruition."

"You're right. My darling husband is so terribly clever."

He chuckled as he yanked her closer. Her face nestled into his chest, and he pressed kisses into her hair. "I forgot to tell you I was followed today."

"The same man?"

"I couldn't see him. It was definitely a different coach. This one was very fine."

Her breath hitched. He had seen her brother's coach. It was a moment before she could form a response. "I think it's very clever of him to try different conveyances to confuse you. You must own, if he followed you in the same conveyance every day, you'd be bound to recognize it, and I doubt he wants that."

"I thought about confronting him."

Her heartbeat roared. She could see that she was going to have to vary her transport. But how? "No! Don't do that. Then those wicked men would know you know about their dishonesty as well as the attack on my cousin. They would almost certainly want to silence you." This seriously frightened her far, far more than the prospect of being discovered following him.

At the notion that Richard's life could be in jeopardy, her eyes moistened, and she wrapped her arms around his torso. "I cannot bear to even think about anything happening to you."

He crushed his lips into hers for a deep, penetrating kiss as his hands glided and kneaded and thoroughly ignited her flames of desire. "May I have Your Grace's permission to relieve you of your clothing?" he asked, his voice husky.

Her hand splayed on his thigh as she inched it upward and answered breathlessly. "Yes, please."

CHAPTER SEVENTEEN

WHEN HER HUSBAND left for Parliament the following day, Emily began to set her new plan into motion. She had learned there was no use sitting in a coach outside of Parliament for hours on end in order to follow him when he left.

"Tell me, Maggie," Emily said to her maid, "where would one go if one wanted to acquire used clothing—something like a flower seller in Covent Garden might wear?"

Maggie looked at her mistress as if she were speaking in a foreign tongue. "Why ever would you want to know somethin' like that?"

Emily regretted she could not be completely honest with her maid. "Actually, I desire to wear them myself. It's for a prank I mean to play on one of my sisters." The gravity of the situation justified her lie.

Also, she had given her word she would not reveal anything about her husband's inquiries into the New Londinium project. To do so could jeopardize her husband's life. Perhaps she would confess the truth whenever this investigation was resolved.

Her stomach tightened at the thought that Devere was still hovering between life and death. She prayed again that he would fully recover. She prayed just as fervently that her husband would stay out of harm's way.

"A fancy lady like yerself probably isn't aware that those

flower sellers possess but one dress."

"What do they wear when it's being washed?"

Maggie glared at her as if she were an imbecile.

Then Emily's mouth dropped open. "Oh. You mean they never wash them?"

With a haughty air, the maid nodded.

"Then I don't suppose I should wish to wear their discarded clothing. Where would I find the type of clothing those women wear?"

"There's a place off Cheapside that's popular with that class of woman."

"Will you show it to me?"

The two decided that Emily might wish to borrow one of Maggie's dresses to wear when they went to Cheapside. "If you go there dressed like a fine duchess, it could be dangerous for you. I wouldn't ride in that coach with yer husband's crest on it, either."

So, within the hour, the two women, dressed similarly in clothes women in service wore, were clopping through the City in James Beresford's coach.

They located the shop on a narrow lane off bustling Cheapside. "You might want to have the coach stop down the street," Maggie advised. "They're not accustomed to having their customers arrive in fine coaches."

When the coachman parked at the end of the street and helped them disembark, Emily noted theirs was the only coach here. "I don't like bringing you to this area, Miss Beresford," the coachman said, his gaze shifting all around, his hand clasping the butt of his musket.

"John, I am no longer Miss Beresford. And I assure you I would not think of coming here without your protection."

She and Maggie walked along the damp pavement. The sun was largely blocked from the narrow lane by the upper floors of the shabby buildings here. The shop Maggie led her to was also dark and narrow.

"Ye better let me do the talking," Maggie said. "You'll stick out like a stain on a fine white gown."

The two walked along the tables that were strewn with second-hand clothing. "I don't want anything too fine," she whispered. "All I ask is that it be clean."

"The proprietor here, I'm told, makes sure all the clothing is washed."

When Maggie held up a high-necked bombazine dress in faded brown, Emily nodded.

"It will be too big for you," Maggie said.

Exactly the look she was striving for. "I will take it. Now, what about boots?" Emily loathed the idea of putting her feet in filthy boots, but she had a part to play and could not compromise on the authentic image she wished to portray.

Maggie fumbled through a pile of boots, none of which could ever have passed for new—and none of which appeared to have been designed for women. However, they were just the sort of footwear she'd seen those women at Covent Garden wear.

"What do you think of these?" Maggie asked, holding up a pair of brown boots that were less worn than most.

Emily held out her foot, attempting to point the sole upward. Maggie held the boot up to her sole. "Close enough."

Though the clothing had been washed and the shoes cleaned of caked mud, a foul odor came from the shoe area. "Let's pay and leave," Emily whispered, handing her reticule to Maggie.

Maggie took care of the transaction, and they left the shop to go back to Mayfair. Instead of going to Grosvenor Square, Emily directed the coachman to take her to Lucy's house on Piccadilly and to deliver Maggie at Bentley House.

She could not let Richard's servants see her dressed as a Covent Garden flower seller, nor could she allow Richard to know it was she who dressed so. She was counting on being able to follow him without him recognizing her. What duke would be paying close attention to an ill-dressed flower woman?

Inside Montague House, she learned that neither Lord nor

Lady Montague was at home. Good. She didn't want anyone she knew to discover her deception.

In her sister's chamber, she dressed in the faded bombazine, which was so large that the shoulder seams hung almost to her elbows, and the skirt dragged on the floor. She borrowed an extra pair of stockings from Lucy's drawer to add an extra layer of protection to her feet when she slipped into the hideous boots.

To make herself look more unrecognizable, she unpinned her hair and allowed it to hang straight and bushy. It was thick enough to obscure part of her face, which is exactly what she wanted.

Lastly, she took a bit of the kohl Lucy rarely used, and she smudged her face to where she resembled a chimney sweep. She stood back and gazed into the looking glass. Any semblance of attractiveness was now gone, and she was certain no one would recognize her. If he didn't look too closely, even her own husband would not recognize her.

AS MUCH AS Bentley had cherished the past two nights with his wife, he felt as if he were swimming upstream in his efforts to reveal who ordered Devere's death. So, when Lord Abbott requested he meet with the committee that night at his house, Bentley hoped this might finally shed some light on what Devere had learned.

Now that Emily knew of his quest, she would understand why he couldn't be with her. He did send around a note to explain that he would not be home that night. The resolution of the New Londinium scheme could not come quickly enough for him. More importantly, he hoped Devere would recover.

During his short journey from the House of Lords to Lord Abbott's, purple shades of dusk darkened to night. At Lord Abbott's, he was greeted by the same group of men he'd met with earlier, and two new ones came. The group must be aggressively seeking to expand. A quick glance around the chamber confirmed that Bentley was still the highest-ranking man there. And likely the wealthiest.

"I've called you gentlemen here tonight," Abbott began, "because it's time we finalize plans."

"Time to show our guineas, eh?" Lord Sloane said with a chuckle.

"Yes, actually," Lord Abbott replied. "In order to get started with all the proper filings, as well as engaging the services of a man of business to oversee this project, we need capital."

"How much of an investment are we expected to make?" asked Samuel Fulton, one of the new members of the group.

Both Abbott and Fletcher shrugged, and Fletcher, who often gave the air of being the group's instigator, answered. "Some may only be able to contribute a few hundred guineas. Others," his glance flicked to Bentley, "will be able to contribute thousands of pounds. At least, that's our hope."

"What of the funds from the government?" Bentley asked, looking directly at Abbott. "Have we found out if this type of investment must be approved by Parliament, or is Lord Abbott authorized to act on behalf of the government?" The biggest danger of the plan was its ability to bankrupt the country, and Bentley wasn't about to let that happen.

Abbott did not answer. When the silence grew awkward, Lord Fletcher stepped in to respond. "I believe Lord Abbott, as Chancellor of the Exchequer, is entrusted with making these types of decisions." His gaze darted to Abbott. "Is that not correct, my lord?"

"That is correct."

"Then you've determined how much the country is going to invest?" Bentley demanded. His gut was swirling under the tension of this confrontation.

It was another moment before Abbott responded. "That is likely to be determined after we know how much we're raising from our organizational committee members, that is you men who are here tonight. That's one of the reasons I've asked you gentlemen to gather this evening. We need a gauge of how much our investors are willing to invest in this promising scheme."

"For the two new members," Lord Fletcher said, "I would like to impress upon them we are promising to pay six percent per annum, beginning in the first year."

"That is most promising," Fulton said.

Bentley did not believe that was achievable, but he wasn't going to keep hammering away at the plan's flaws. At least, not yet.

But how was he to leave here tonight without pledging a hefty sum to their shaky scheme when he had no intention of investing in it?

It made sense to him that one of these three founders of the group—Abbott, Fletcher, or Sloane—must be responsible for the attack on Devere. They stood to gain the most, or potentially lose the most, depending on the outcome of the scheme. But which one would actually do it? He had difficulty believing their Chancellor of the Exchequer could be working against the country he had served for so long.

That left Fletcher and Sloane. He kept thinking about what Rockingham had said about Fletcher's wickedness while a student at Eton, but boys' pranks should not follow them to taint their adult lives. Still, what he had done to the Woolley lad was a vile thing to do. What if the tendency toward cruel pranks in the boy had turned into something more sinister in the man? As to Sloane, Bentley could not dismiss that Sloane might very well be desperate for money and could have considered Devere a threat to implementing their plan.

Niggling at the back of his brain, he kept wondering if all three men were knowingly setting out to defraud their country and their friends or if they were simply foolish or misled themselves. He had difficulty believing the three of them could be responsible for a scheme they had to know was doomed to failure.

"Since it's not yet time for the quarter," Lord Crawford said, "many of us aren't in a position to come up with funds at this time. Am I correct in assuming what you need tonight is merely a pledge?"

As a man of honor, Bentley had never in his life made a pledge he did not fulfill, and he had no intentions of fulfilling a pledge to contribute to this questionable scheme. It bothered him to sign his name to a lie, but if he could prove evil-doing against Devere, that should release him and all the others from their pledges. All the more reason why he must expose this deceit and murderous intent.

"That's correct," Lord Abbott said. "And because some of us are more affluent than others, we'll write down our commitments. These will be seen only by the three of us founding members: myself, Lord Fletcher, and Lord Sloane. By making a pledge, you will be agreeing also to allow us to use your name for advertisements to solicit new investors. Is everyone all right with that?" He gazed around the chamber, but no one made any objection.

"Before we make pledges, we will be happy to answer any questions at all you might have about the New Londinium stock offering," Lord Abbott said.

"So you're saying you won't need the money until the next quarter?" Mr. Cookson asked.

"That's right," Lord Fletcher said. "It's just a little over a month away."

Bentley was once more questioning the government's involvement in the scheme. "I know you're the expert on our country's treasury, Lord Abbott, but I don't know how we can secure funds from the government as soon as the next quarter. Won't that have to be built into the budget for next year?"

"That's right, Your Grace. I'm working on that now."

"Are you in a position to be able to pledge a certain amount from the government?" Bentley asked.

"I am."

Bentley's chest tightened. "May I inquire how much?"

"The, ah, final amount is yet to be determined."

Bentley wanted to question Abbott further, but he knew he was treading on very thin ice. If only he knew how far Devere had pushed.

Lord Sloane then passed around a printed page that pledged funds for the New Londinium Committee and had blank spaces for the donor's signature as well as for the amount of that person's pledge.

"You can fold these over and set them on the table here," Sloane instructed. "Then, if it's agreeable to Lord Abbott, you're free to leave." He eyed their host, who nodded.

"By the way," Fulton said, "I went by to inquire on Lord Devere's recovery today." He frowned. "The poor fellow's taken a turn for the worse. Might not make it." He glanced at Bentley. "I understand he's now your kinsman since you married into the Beresford family."

All the men in the chamber were staring at him. Bentley's gut plunged. Just as troubling as the news of Devere's setback was the knowledge that he would now be linked to Devere. He and Emily could possibly be in danger. Still, he would never deny his marriage.

"I didn't know you'd wed the Beresford beauty," Lord Fletcher said.

Bentley shrugged. "Given the tragedy with her cousin, we've not been in a celebratory mood."

"Felicitations and all that, old fellow," Lord Sloane said.

Others in the chamber extended their congratulations, then one by one they stepped up to the table and used the pen there to fill in their sheets of paper.

Bentley pledged ten thousand, the same amount of Emily's dowry—the dowry he hadn't wanted to accept—which was the most generous dowry he knew of. Then he said his farewells and left, disappointed that he'd made no more progress in identifying the person responsible for wanting Devere dead and even more disappointed they'd learned he was now related to Devere.

OWING TO THE choking traffic on the city's streets at the time the House of Lords finished that day, Emily was able to follow her husband on foot when Parliament released at twilight. He went to Lord Abbott's on Cavendish Square where many other men were gathering. Dressed in her shabby flower-selling garb, she stood at the entrance to the square that was closest to the West End's shops and made an effort to appear to be hawking flowers.

She chastised herself for not wearing a warmer coat. Because she'd been standing outside the Palace of Westminster under bright, sunny skies, she'd only tossed on a red knit shawl. But now that it was night, she was miserably cold. She longed to stuff her frozen fingers into her ermine muff or to be within Lord Abbott's cozy house instead of standing out in the elements on this cold, windy night.

While stationing herself on that corner, she tried to come up with a method to more thoroughly investigate Lords Sloane and Fletcher. One of them had wanted to kill her cousin, and she would do anything to uncover which of them was responsible.

As she was pondering this, the same coach that had been previously following her husband turned onto Cavendish Square. Richard was not likely to notice it, given that all the men now gathering at Lord Abbott's had coaches waiting in front of every house on the square.

All of a sudden, an idea occurred to her, an idea that could quite possibly lead to finding out who wanted Devere dead.

Chapter Eighteen

FOR A WOMAN who was credited with being intelligent, Emily was furious with herself for her stupidity. The absence of a warm coat was not as infuriating as her lack of transportation. Just because she'd been able to follow a coach on foot at dusk when streets were clogged with conveyances did not mean she would be able to follow a coach when night cleared those same streets.

Lacking transportation, she had another idea.

She was thankful it was a moonless night. She was also thankful her brown dress rather blended in with the darkness. Moving as silently as possible, she began to walk toward that shabby coach, the one used by the man following her husband.

When she reached it, she waited behind it for a few moments to make sure no one had seen or heard her. She was in luck. In addition to no one noticing her, she discovered a rack at the back of the coach where she could steal away and follow the follower. Because her dress and hair were dark, she prayed she would not be noticed on this exceptionally dark night.

The man inside would be sure to feel it when she put her weight on the back of the coach. She would have to climb on at the very moment the coach sprang forward.

She did not have to wait very long before men began leaving Lord Abbott's house. Her husband was the third to leave. She had a very good idea that she would soon know where he was going because she was almost positive the coach she was stealing away on was going to follow him.

The second her husband's coach turned off Cavendish Square, the coach she intended to climb upon spurted forward. She leapt on it and held on tightly as it picked up speed. By poking her head so she could see around the back of the coach, she saw Richard's coach. It was moving toward Grosvenor Square.

Her heart sank. He was coming home to be with her, but she wasn't going to be there. She had other plans tonight, plans she hoped would bring to justice the person responsible for the attack on her cousin.

Just as she thought, the coach she was riding on was following Richard. After he disembarked from his coach and entered their house, the man inside the coach told his driver, "That will be all for tonight. The bloke won't be coming out no more. Take mc back to Spitalfields."

She hoped she would get home in time to spend the night with Richard.

The coach left the West End and drove down the Strand. This busy street was still bustling with coaches, saddle horses, pedestrians, and queues of people trying to get in shops that were open still.

Minutes later, they were in the City where there were more pedestrians than horses or horse-driven vehicles. It was much darker here, too. Quiet streets where formidable bank buildings that had closed hours earlier gave way to narrower lanes where laughter rang from boisterous public houses, babes cried in overcrowded tenements, and gatherings of warmly bundled men reminded her there were still many hours left of this night.

The farther east they went, the lower the class of people was. In her present state of dress, she would fit right in. Even so, she regretted she had no weapon.

She possessed something else, something she believed would

prove more important than a weapon. She meant to bargain with the follower. The follower must have also been involved in the theft and murder attempt at Devere House on the evening of her wedding.

Someone who was powerful on the New Londinium Committee had ordered Devere's murder, and she was convinced that same person also would have used the services of his hired thieves and assassins to follow her husband.

Because of the darkness and because she was so unfamiliar with the places they were passing, she realized she had no knowledge of the place—Spitalfields—where they were going, and she would be hard pressed to find her way back to the familiar comfort of the West End. But they had not gone so far that they were in the country. These streets were crowded with skinny house after skinny house—none of them particularly nice.

Soon the coach stopped, and the follower got out. "We'll see you tomorrow, same time," he said to the driver.

Emily stepped off the coach, but not as quietly as she would have liked. The follower turned around and stared at her. "You following me?"

"As a matter of fact, I am." As soon as the words were out of her mouth, she regretted them. She really was in want of a brain. She had spoken in her cultured voice instead of the voice of a flower seller. It was too late now to go back. "I'm here to offer you a handsome reward for certain information."

Owing to the darkness, she could not see the expression on his face, but she could tell he was looking her up and down as if he were trying to determine what breed of woman she was. He did not respond for a moment.

What was going through his mind? Was she in danger?

"Come inside, and we'll discuss it." Unlike her, his voice was of the lower classes.

Her breath halted in her chest. She felt far safer standing here on the street than she would in his residence. This man was apt to want to take liberties with her. What a pity she had no weapon.

She could not turn back now. She doubted he would allow that. Since he had already heard her cultured voice, she saw no reason to change it now. Besides, a woman who spoke like her would be expected to possess some wealth. "As you must have realized, I am in disguise. My . . . husband will be here soon." He must believe she was not an unprotected woman.

"I didn't see no one following us."

"My husband . . ." What? What could she say? She had to hope he was as stupid as she was acting. "Knows things."

"Who is your husband?"

"I'm not at liberty to say. I dare say he will let you know when the time comes."

"Will my lady come this way?" He swept into a gallant bow though there was only malice in his voice.

Trembling, she followed him into the slender house where lights shone in the window. She was disappointed to learn they wouldn't be alone. Or maybe there would be safety in numbers for her. Another man who stank of gin was in the candlelit room they entered.

The floors here were uncovered, well-worn wood, and the only furnishings consisted of a pair of rickety-looking wooden chairs. It was obvious the shabby lodgings lacked a woman's touch.

"Buyin' flowers, Jacob?" the large man whose front tooth was missing said to the man who accompanied her.

"No, this 'ere's a proper lady, though she don't look like it." Jacob looked at her. "Say somethin', my lady."

Her heart roared in her ears, and she could not stop trembling, yet she cautioned herself to be brave. Her gaze went from one man to the other. "I believe you are the men responsible for the theft at Lord Devere's house a few days ago. I'm not here to reprimand you. I'm here to learn who put you up to the commission of the crime, and I'm willing to pay for the information. I don't know who you are, nor do I want to accuse you of any crime. I only want to know the identity of the person who hired you."

The man with the missing tooth came closer to her. "How much are you willing to pay?"

Her gaze once more bounced from one to the other. "I am prepared to pay one hundred guineas."

"Let me see yer money." It appeared the toothless man was the leader here, rather than Jacob the Follower.

With trembling hands, she dropped her bunch of flowers—why she'd brought them all this way was beyond her comprehension, foolish woman—and held up her reticule, shaking it so its gold coins jingled.

The huge, hulking man snatched it from her and dumped the coins into his huge hands. His eyes flashed with mirth.

"Now you have the money," she said. "I want the information."

He looked her in the eye. The man was more than a head taller than her. "The person who hired us paid more handsomely." He looked at Jacob. "I wonder how much he'll pay to get his hands on this here woman?"

A jolt of fear walloped her. This was not what she had planned. "Give me back my money!"

Both men burst into guffaws of laughter. When he stopped laughing, the toothless man looked at Jacob. "Tie the woman up."

WHERE WAS HIS wife? Bentley had been happy to make it home in time to spend the rest of the evening with Emily, but she wasn't there. Then he recalled Fulton telling them Devere had taken a turn for the worse. Of course, she would be at Devere House.

He hoped to God her cousin hadn't died.

He sped around to the mews before the tack had been removed from his matched horses, even before they'd been unhitched from the coach, and directed his coachman to take him to Devere's house.

At Devere House, he was met with the long faces of Devere's family members. He did not at first see Emily. "How is Devere?" he asked, dreading the bad news that was almost certain to be delivered.

James spoke. "Not as good as we had hoped. The surgeon is now saying he might not recover."

At that, Harriett Rockingham broke into tears. Her husband moved to comfort her.

Bentley's hands fisted. He was more determined than ever to expose the person responsible for this. If Devere should die, Bentley would make sure everyone knew the Earl of Devere had sacrificed his life for Britain. Bentley's lids lowered as he solemnly shook his head.

All the Beresfords and their spouses were here, except for his wife—and Lady Devere, who still refused to leave her husband's side. Emily must have entered the sick room.

Once Harriett's cries subsided, her husband spoke to Bentley. "May I have a word, Your Grace?"

The two men went to Devere's library where Lord Rockingham poured two glasses of brandy.

"Wretched news about Devere," Bentley said, shaking his head.

"We've all been sick with worry." Rockingham handed one of the glasses to Bentley. "Let's drink to Devere's recovery."

Their glasses clanked together, and they swigged.

"I thought you weren't coming to Devere House anymore. What's changed?"

Bentley frowned. "Samuel Fulton showed up at a New Londinium Committee meeting at Lord Abbott's tonight and told the whole lot of them that I'd married a Beresford. I could hardly deny it."

Rockingham winced. "Makes the going much tougher for you."

"Indeed it does."

"I don't suppose you've learned anything yet about who ordered that Devere be killed?"

"Nothing, unfortunately."

"I know it's difficult for you without knowing what Devere had learned. I just wish he'd shared his suspicions with me from the beginning."

Bentley gave a bitter laugh. "As I wish. Desperately."

"And you're still not favorably impressed with the merits of the New Londinium scheme?"

"The more I know, the more I know how thoroughly it's doomed to fail."

"Which is obviously what Devere learned."

"Poor Devere. There are a lot of people praying for him."

"Our wives went to St. George's to pray."

"Speaking of our wives, is mine in the sick room with Lady Devere?"

Rockingham's brows scrunched together. "No. She's not here."

Bentley's heartbeat thudded. Inexplicably, he felt something was gravely wrong. Everyone she was close to in the Capital was in this house right now. Who else could she possibly be with? And why was she not home for dinner?

"Was she here earlier?" Perhaps they'd passed in the night.

"To my knowledge, she's not been here since this morning."

Filled with dread, Bentley finished off his brandy and stood. "Perhaps she's home now. I must go see."

Though it was only a few moments, the drive home seemed interminable. At Bentley House, he raced up the stairs and threw open the door to Emily's chamber. She was not there, and there were no signs that she had been there. He walked to her dressing chamber. It, too, was empty. With renewed hope, he rushed to his own bedchamber, the place where they had come together for sublime lovemaking. He threw open the door—only to be crushed when he saw she did not occupy the dark chamber, either.

Where in the devil could she be? It was getting later and later. He vowed to stay awake until she came home.

Chapter Nineteen

The gin-stinking man tied her wrists and ankles together. Tightly. She was so upset, she discounted the pain where the rough rope cut into her flesh. One could hardly dwell on discomfort when one's very life was at stake. These men had been hired to kill Devere. She would be their second victim.

Nausea rose, her heartbeat pounded and thumped, and she cursed herself for stupidity. How could she have been so lacking in intelligence? If she screamed as loudly as she could, would anyone even come? She let out a shrill scream, and Toothless clamped his filthy hand over her mouth. "Get something to gag this woman."

A moment later, a nasty-smelling rag was tied around her mouth.

Toothless then directed his attention at Jacob. "You better consult with our fancy lord to see what he wants us to do with her."

"He's not due here until tomorrow morning."

It sounded to her as if they might not know the identity of the man orchestrating the evil-doings. He had not been referred to by name, nor did they seem to know where they could find him, though he obviously knew how to find them.

"Didn't she say her husband would soon be here?" Jacob said.

If only.

"I think she was bluffin'. Look at her hand. I don't see no ring," said the big, toothless fellow.

Of course she wouldn't have worn her emerald and diamond wedding ring while dressed as a poor flower seller!

Jacob's gaze shifted from her bound hands to the man who ordered him about. "I know she don't look it, but I think she might be a fine lady. Her husband could be someone real important."

Toothless strode to her and lifted her hands. "These do be the hands of a lady, but if her husband was going to be here, he would already have come. We'll see what our leader lord has to say."

Once more, this man had failed to call the lord by name. It was understandable that the man responsible for the attack on Devere wanted to keep his identity a secret. All of the three suspects were powerful Tories. And one of them was a killer. She thought it must be Lord Sloane. But, then again, it could be Lord Fletcher. But she did not think their Chancellor of the Exchequer could possibly be a party to harming his country's treasury.

Jacob was staring at her. "I think if she cleaned up, she would look good." His searing gaze raked over her.

Thankfully, with the ill-fitting clothes and the kohl smudged on her face, she did not believe she looked in any way desirable. Her breath hitched in her chest. At least she hoped she didn't. She would be powerless to fight off any advances from these disgusting men.

Death might be preferable.

"We'll wait to hear from our leader lord before we decide what to do with her," the toothless leader said. "For now, lock her in the bedchamber that's got no windows."

Jacob looked perplexed. "I don't know which chamber that be."

Toothless glared. "It ain't got no bed in it now, but it was a bedchamber."

"Oh, I know which one, then." Jacob stepped forward and

lifted her, throwing her over his shoulder as if she were a rolled-up carpet. "I'll need a candle."

Toothless sighed. "I'll walk wiv you."

With the lighted candlestick showing them the way, they mounted a dark, narrow staircase that led to two rooms. Jacob tossed her in the one to the left. There was nothing, not even a wooden chair, in the chamber. Then they closed the door, and a key twisted in the lock. She was in complete darkness.

Sickness rising from the pit of her stomach, she believed she'd be dead by this time tomorrow. Life obviously was not important to their so-called leader lord, or he would not have ordered the stabbing of her cousin.

Her own stupidity had gotten her into this lethal situation. By acting alone, she'd ensured her own demise. No one outside of this house knew where she was. There was no way Richard could ever find her.

WHEN BENTLEY RETURNED home, he went to his wife's bedchamber and rang for her maid.

"Do you know where the duchess has gone?" he asked.

"I don't, and I'm a wee bit alarmed. Haven't seen her since she went off midday to dress in those horrid clothes. I thought she'd be back in an hour or two, but she's never returned."

"What do you mean by those *horrid clothes*?"

"She wanted to dress like one of them flower sellers at Covent Garden."

"Where in the devil did my wife get her hands on something like that?"

"I accompanied her to a place off Cheapside where she purchased them—or rather, I did for her. Later, she was planning to wear them."

"Here?"

"No. She didn't want you or yer servants to see her, so she went to her sister's. Lady Montague's."

"Why, pray tell, did my wife wish to look like a flower seller?"

"She said she was playing a lark on her sister. Why ever, I cannot imagine."

Bentley didn't believe that for a moment. Her disguise had to have something to do with his inquiries. The maddening woman was obviously planning her own surveillance.

He felt as if he'd been kicked in the gut. She must have been discovered. And dealt with.

As worried as he'd been about Devere, he was a thousand times more worried now. He thanked the maid and raced back downstairs, leaving by the back door to once again try to use his coach before the horses had been unhitched.

Moments later, he was rushing into Devere House. The first person he saw was Lady Montague. "Did my wife play a prank on you today?" he demanded.

She looked puzzled. "What kind of prank?"

"Never mind." Bentley turned away, searching for his wife's other sister. He prayed he was wrong, prayed that Emily had played a jest on Lady Churston. She sat near the fire, next to her husband.

Bentley was always struck by how much Emily and Lady Churston resembled each other, but now that he knew his wife so intimately, he distinguished the subtle differences between them, realized Emily had more curves than her sister, though both were slender. The very thought of those luscious curves made him all the more melancholy.

"Tell me, Lady Churston, did my wife play a hoax on you today?"

She glared. "She did not. I'm out of charity with Emily, if you must know. She should be here with her family at this difficult time, and heaven knows where she is."

He wished to God he did know where she was. He prayed she would not end up like Devere. He swallowed over the nausea that mushroomed inside him.

So Georgiana Churston was angry with Emily, too, but for completely different reasons. He was furious with his wife. Why could she not have agreed to his requests to stay out of the investigation?

Terrified something terrible had happened to her, he stormed from the house. He had no idea how to find his wife, but he knew her absence had to be tied to his investigation. Therefore, the man who ordered Devere's death would also order hers. A sickening dread slammed through him. She might already be dead.

Even though he wasn't sure where he would go or what he would do, he knew he would need to be armed. Back at his house, he donned boots and slipped a sheathed knife into them. Then he strapped on his sword and hurried to his waiting coach. "Back to Cavendish Square," he ordered.

The time for pretense was over. He would confess everything and enlist Lord Abbott's help to find his wife. After all, Abbott was one of the highest-ranking men in the British government.

Fortunately, Abbott was at home. "Please tell Lord Abbott that the Duke of Bedford begs a private word with him," Bentley said.

He was shown to the library, and a few moments later a smiling Lord Abbott entered. "To what do I owe the pleasure, Your Grace?" When he saw the angry look on his visitor's face, his expression changed.

Bentley, his hands fisted, his eyes icy, said, "I need your help. Forgive me for not previously being honest with you. I expressed interest in the New Londinium scheme at the behest of Lord Devere. He believed, er, believes, that the theft at his home was subterfuge to cover up the real motive: someone wanted him dead because he was going to expose the flaws in the New Londinium project."

Abbott's brows lowered. "You must be mistaken. I can't believe any of these honorable men would order another peer's death."

"Right now, I believe my wife's life is in danger."

"The Beresford girl?"

"The Duchess of Bentley, yes. She has been trying to help me find out who's responsible for the attack on her cousin, Devere—against my wishes. I believe she may have been captured." He swallowed hard. "Or worse."

"These are preposterous accusations. Who do you think capable of such evil?"

Bentley shrugged. "My guess is either Lord Fletcher or Lord Sloane. I'm desperate to know which one. I need you to aid me in finding my wife."

"I have difficulty believing your story, but I'll do everything in my power to help you find your wife." He walked to the desk and scribbled a note. "In my official capacity, I'm writing to the Duke of York to request that the Horse Guards be pressed into service to assist us." After he sealed the note, he rang for a servant, and when the servant came, he told him to deliver it. "We'll go confront Sloane and Fletcher. I believe they're together tonight." His gaze went to Bentley's sword. "I see you're ready for possible violence."

"I am."

"I'll just go fetch my sword. Won't be a minute." After he left, Bentley heard muffled men's voices coming from the entry corridor, followed by the opening of the front door.

It was at least five minutes later before the Chancellor of the Exchequer returned, sporting a sword. "By the way, to save time since I know how anxious you are, I had my footman tell your coachman our destination."

As they left his home, Abbott asked Bentley, "So what makes you think either Lord Sloane or Lord Fletcher might be responsible for the injury to your wife's kinsman?"

"I cannot say with any authority, but I was told that Sloane has met with some large losses at Newmarket. I would think that would make it more imperative that he raise money from the

New Londinium scheme."

Lord Abbott nodded. "It's true. His losses were substantial. And Fletcher? Why do you suspect him?"

Bentley did not like to spread gossip. If Fletcher proved to be innocent, he did not wish to tarnish his name or reputation. He was a well-respected Tory lawmaker. He shrugged. "It may be nothing, but I've been told he was guilty of a vile deed whilst a student at Eton." He glanced at Lord Abbott as that man held open the coach door for him. "I know lads do many things they later regret."

Inside Bentley's coach, the men faced each other. "Indeed. I would hate any of my boyhood pranks to revisit me now," Lord Abbott said with a little laugh.

"I concur."

With every churn of the wheels, Bentley grew more worried about Emily. Lord Abbott was uncharacteristically rattling on, but Bentley was too upset to follow along attentively.

"I thought you a confirmed bachelor, Your Grace."

"As did I," Bentley said. "Until I met Emily Beresford."

"I've never had the pleasure of meeting her, but I'm told she's quite lovely."

"I believe so, but there were other qualities that elevated her over every other woman I've ever known." His heart softened as he recalled his wife's many attributes which had initially attracted him. When he recalled her infinite capacity for passion, he almost broke down.

"The Beresfords are without a doubt one of England's oldest and most respected families. Pity about Lord Devere. I understand he may not make it."

The very thought of Devere's death—and possibly Emily's, too—sliced through Bentley like a blazing sword. His lips folded into a grim line. "Whoever is responsible will pay."

"Agreed." Abbott shook his head forlornly. "I just can't believe either Lord Fletcher or Lord Sloane could be capable of . . . murder."

It seemed to Bentley they should already have arrived at the Horse Guards. "Where did you say Lords Fletcher and Sloane are tonight?"

Lord Abbott did not answer for a moment. "Uh, I can't remember the name of the place, but we'll be there shortly."

As the coach rattled along the streets, Lord Abbott kept babbling.

Bentley felt something was wrong—other than the almost-certain danger that faced his wife. During the entire coach ride, something had been niggling at his subconscious.

All of a sudden, he realized what was askew. He never saw his coachman when they left Abbott House. He recalled Abbott saying he'd sent his footman to disclose their destination to his coachman.

But it was Abbott himself who had held open the coach door for Bentley. That was a function always performed by his coachman. And Abbott had spoken every second since closing the door of Abbott House. Was he trying to distract Bentley?

Had Abbott ordered that something be done to his coachman? Installed his own servant?

That could mean Bentley was wrong about everything. It wasn't Fletcher or Sloane who'd ordered Devere's death.

It was Lord Abbott.

Right now, this coach must be carrying him to the place where Emily had been taken, the place where the hired cutthroats were located. If he had any hope of saving his wife—or himself—during the remainder of this ride he must not reveal his suspicions. He must act the complete pawn of the deranged chancellor.

It was imperative that the very instant the coach halted, he be ready.

As badly as he wanted to run his sword through Abbott, he forced himself to appear to be eagerly listening to the man's every word.

"I must say, Bentley, I'm exceedingly disappointed to hear

that you believe our New Londinium Committee is misguided, but I will own that I may have put too much trust in Lords Sloane and Fletcher. As you know, I'm a very busy man."

"I do understand that, my lord." *You're a greedy, vile, murderer.* "It's just a good thing we've caught them at their corrupt game before any harm was done." That much was true.

Bentley's insides churned with every turn of the coach wheels. They had long ago passed the Horse Guards, passed the old City, and, if he was not mistaken, they were now in one of those undesirable boroughs of the East End. He prayed he wouldn't be too late.

If something had happened to Emily . . . it was too painful to contemplate.

"Indeed, it is."

"I suppose you've asked the Horse Guards to meet us where Lords Sloane and Fletcher are?" *You lying, cheating criminal.*

"Oh, yes. I expect they'll be there when we arrive. By the way, Your Grace, I have not offered my felicitations on your nuptials."

Bentley forced a smile. "Thank you, my lord. I am the most fortunate of men." It was obvious to him that Abbott was running out of comments and wished to keep the conversation going to divert Bentley's attention.

The coach turned off a busy street onto a quiet lane. He dared not look out the window, dared not allow Lord Abbott to know of his suspicions. The coach slowed.

He was ready.

Chapter Twenty

SMILING AND NODDING at Lord Abbott, Bentley lowered his hand into his boot as if he were going to scratch his ankle and quickly unsheathed his knife, whipped it out, and lunged across the coach to hold the knife to the chancellor's throat.

Terror transformed Abbott's face. "What the devil?"

"You will tell your minions to do as I say, or I'll kill you." Those were words Bentley never thought he would ever utter. Equally as shocking, he fully intended to carry through with his threat if Abbott didn't comply.

The coachman jumped off the box and sped around to open the door. Just as Bentley expected, it wasn't his own coachman. It was Abbott's burly footman. The man's frightened gaze went from the knife poised at his master's neck to Bentley.

"Do as this man says," Abbott instructed his servant.

"Yes, my lord." The footman's gaze shifted to Bentley.

"Open the door on this side of the carriage," Bentley commanded.

Once his door was open, Bentley ordered the footman to get back up on the box, then Bentley backed away from the coach and withdrew his sword. "You will leave by this door now, Lord Abbott." Without removing his gaze from the chancellor, he took note of his surroundings.

This dark street appeared to have derelict houses, but a light shone in the window of the skinny terrace house they had stopped in front of. He prayed Emily was here.

"You never let on that you suspected me," Abbott said, somberly shaking his head.

"I didn't suspect you. It wasn't until I figured out we weren't going to the Horse Guards that I recalled you talking to someone just outside your library and heard your entry door open. That's when I suspected you may have switched drivers." He hoped his family's long-time coachman was not hurt, but the focus of his attention now needed to be on finding Emily. He prayed it wasn't too late.

"And I thought I'd fooled you."

"Neither Devere nor I are fools. Now, I suggest you knock on that door. My sword will be at your back, and if you make a false move, I swear it will spear through your heart."

The two moved slowly to the front door near the lighted window. Abbott rapped at the door. The wiry, dark-haired man who answered it was the man who had been following Bentley, he was almost certain.

Recognition and surprise registered on the man's face when he saw Lord Abbott. "My lord! To what do we owe this visit?" His follower's glance flicked to Bentley, and a quizzing expression flashed across his face.

Instead of receiving a reply from Abbott, Bentley answered. "If you want to ensure your employer stays alive, you will bring me the woman."

"What woman?"

Bentley tensed. He'd been counting on Emily being here. Where was she? "The one dressed as a flower seller."

By then, another man came to the door. This unshaven man, who was missing a front tooth, was huge.

"Is this that lord you've been meeting with, Jacob?" the large man asked the smaller one.

"Yes. And he's being threatened by the bloke I've been following."

The large man's gaze went to Bentley's sword.

"All I want," Bentley said as he urged the chancellor forward and the two men entered the dwelling, "is the woman. Produce her, and I'll leave."

"Go on upstairs and get the woman," the large man commanded. The man named Jacob picked up a lighted candle and complied.

She's alive! Bentley's entire body uncoiled from the knots it had been tied in for the past hour.

Bentley's relief was short lived.

A moment later, Jacob descended the stairs, a knife leveled at Emily's throat. Her hands were tied, her mouth bound. Rope dangled from her ankles. It had been slashed, presumably so she could walk down the stairs while her captor held the knife to her neck. Even in the wretched garb and with a blackened face, she was his beautiful Emily. And she was unharmed. So far.

Bentley's gaze shifted to a smirking Abbott.

"May I suggest Your Grace drop his sword unless you want to see your wife's lovely throat cut?" Abbott said.

What an evil man Abbott was! Bentley eyed his terrified wife and dropped both sword and knife. Now that he was unarmed, Abbott drew his sword from the scabbard.

"Kill her anyway!" Abbott commanded.

Emily froze in terror.

A frightened look swiped across Jacob's face. He shook his head. "I've done some bad things, but I ain't gonna kill no woman." He looked at his partner in crime.

"I think, you fine lord," the huge man said to Abbott, "we will just take the hundred pounds the lady gave us and leave you to this killin'." His gaze connected with Jacob's, and he nodded.

The two men, both with knives drawn, edged toward the front door and then walked away, leaving the door open behind them.

During the second when Abbott's gaze flicked to his hired henchmen, Bentley swiftly stooped to pick up his sword. Now that it was one-on-one, Bentley stood a chance. More than a chance. He was probably twenty years younger than Abbott and was credited to be a fine swordsman.

He leapt back, one foot lunging forward, sword drawn, facing Abbott. Without his pair of lawbreakers, Abbott looked lost. And old. His frightened gaze shifted to Bentley's sword, and he, too, moved into his fencing stance, rapier locking with Bentley's.

The two parried several times, each time Bentley driving his opponent backward a little more. Abbott's motions were no match for the younger man's swift attack. He began to purposely move them from the house.

Bentley had never killed anyone before, and he had no interest in killing anyone tonight. But killing Abbott right now would be as easy as a blink.

With one powerful swipe, he knocked away Abbott's rapier.

Terror in his eyes, Abbott gasped, then began to cry, whimpering as he said, "I beg you. Spare me."

Bentley kicked away Abbott's sword. "Love?" he said to Emily. "Can you use his sword to cut away those ropes from your hands?"

She freed herself from the tightly tied rope.

"Get in the coach," Bentley ordered Abbott.

A tearful Emily was just behind them. She had picked up his knife. "You, too, my love. I'll take that knife."

Once he had the knife, he asked her to sheath his sword in his scabbard.

Without removing Abbott from his line of sight, Bentley turned his attention to Abbott's footman. "What have you done with my coachman?"

The youthful man did not answer for a moment. "My lord told me to knock him out, so I did. Then I tied him up and left him in the mews."

Bentley prayed the coachman would be all right. "You're to drive us to Cavendish Square," Bentley ordered the footman.

The Duke and Duchess of Bentley then sat across the coach

from the weeping Lord Abbott. "My dear wife, will you take that rope from your ankles and tie the man's hands together?"

Five minutes into the journey, Lord Abbott said, "May I inquire as to why your duchess . . . appears as she does?"

Both he and Emily burst into laughter. "Is it not obvious she did not wish to be recognized?" Bentley said.

Not for one second during the half-an-hour, predawn drive did the duke remove his gaze or the aim of his knife from the vile man who sat across from him.

ENSCONCED IN THE library at Abbott House, Bentley demanded at knifepoint that the chancellor write a letter disclosing his sham stock plan and his attempt on Lord Devere's life. Once the ink on the letter was blotted and the confession sealed with Abbott's stamp, Bentley said, "I will give you a choice, my lord. You can stand trial in the House of Lords, or you will leave the country today." He knew which one the chancellor would select.

"I will have to withdraw funds before I can leave the country."

"No. You will leave now. I suspect some of those funds you wish to withdraw have been stolen from our country's treasury."

Abbott directed a look of pure hatred at him.

"Tell me, Abbott, how do Lords Fletcher and Sloane figure into your scheme?"

Abbott shook his head. "They don't. They're fools I can easily manipulate."

"Unlike Devere?"

Abbott nodded mournfully. "I had to have him eliminated."

"If he dies, you will pay," Bentley said. He then turned to his wife. "My love, I shall need you to find Lord Rockingham and ask him to come here."

While he waited for Emily to return from dispatching a

footman, Bentley said a prayer of thanks that Emily had not been harmed. Or killed. A few hours had likely meant the difference between her living and dying. If he had not picked up on Abbott's guilt when he did, he believed Abbott would have killed her today.

Even the thought of it upset him.

Rockingham soon arrived. "Her Grace has apprised me of last night's occurrence and of Lord Abbott's guilt," Rockingham said. "So, he's decided to leave the country?"

"Indeed." Bentley's gaze flicked to the sealed letter. "Since the duchess and I have been up all night, we're asking that you see Lord Abbott to Dover. You will, of course, have to be armed."

Rockingham eyed the disgraced Chancellor of the Exchequer. "It will be my pleasure to get this rubbish out of England."

A SLIPPER TUB of warm water had been brought to Richard's bedchamber and placed in front of the fire. He helped Emily from the too-large bombazine that had disguised her the previous day. He had knelt at her feet and removed the hideous boots and both pairs of stockings.

"I ought to be scolding you for almost getting yourself killed," Richard said. "I begged you to stay out of my investigation."

As she lowered into the soothing water, she looked into that face she loved so thoroughly. "You were worried about me."

"I have never in my life been more terrified than I was last night." He knelt alongside the tub and trickled water over her bare shoulders.

"Sorrows remembered strengthen present joy. I do understand how you felt last night, my darling. That's why I felt compelled to aid in your clandestine activities. I was worried sick that you would be killed, like they tried to do to Devere." She clasped a hand over his. "I wouldn't want to live in a world void of you."

He swallowed and spoke in a husky whisper. "I feel the same." He moistened and soaped a cloth and began to try to remove the black smudges from her pretty face. "What the devil did you put on your face? Coal from the fireplace?"

"No, silly. It's kohl."

"That's what I said!"

No. K-O-H-L. it's something women use around the eyes. It's more popular in the Orient and India."

"I'm glad my beautiful wife does not live in the Orient. I love your face just as it was." He lathered the soap and wiped away the last of the kohl, and then peered closely at her. "As it is again." He pressed a light kiss on her clean cheek, then he slickened his hands with more foaming soap and glided his magical hands along the length of her arms, the caressed her breasts.

"Do you know, my darling, I thought we were both going to be killed back there at that horrid house. Even after those men—who weren't so very wretched, after all—left, I feared that wicked Lord Abbott would drive his sword through you. I've never been so terrified. Not even when that man named Jacob pointed the knife at my throat."

"You needn't have worried about me. At least, not after the two henchmen left. Abbott's an old man. He didn't stand a chance against me."

She looked up into his beloved face. A day's growth of very dark beard shadowed his angular cheeks. No one had ever looked manlier. "I should pity any man who would have to go up against my rugged husband." Just being so close to him filled her with desire. "My virile husband," she said in a throaty voice.

He groaned.

"Get the towel, my love," she said. "I'm ready." Their eyes met, and he nodded.

When she stepped from the tub and into the towel, he wrapped his arms around her and carried her to the bed.

Lying side by side on the bed, she looked into his eyes and

teared up. "I never dreamed yesterday you'd ever find me. I truly thought I would die in that house, and I believe I would have if you, my hero, hadn't come."

He pulled her close and held her tightly. "Wherever you would go, I will find you." Then his lips pressed against hers for a tender kiss. "I will love you until the day of our death, and then I will love you beyond the grave."

EPILOGUE

Devere House, one month later

NO ONE OBSERVING the Earl of Devere would ever guess that weeks earlier he'd been facing death. The very day Lord Rockingham had escorted the wicked Lord Abbott to a packet boat at Dover, Emily's ailing cousin had sat up in bed and called for the Duke of Bentley.

By the following day, the London newspapers had gotten ahold of the news about the treachery of the former Chancellor of the Exchequer, and the Earl of Devere and the Duke of Bentley were being toasted throughout the Capital as heroes.

With all the publicity, the marriage of the Duke and Duchess of Bentley was no longer a secret. It seemed as if everyone in London had sent felicitations on their marriage.

Because the Duke of Bentley was now known to have married a Beresford, the newspapers were full of accounts of the various investigations and subsequent resolutions of what the newsmen were now referring to as the "Beresford Adventures." This was the fourth so-called Beresford Adventure in just under one year.

Devere detested such publicity.

Tonight, Devere had invited all the family remaining in London to dinner. Emily's whole family was there, except for James, who had returned to Tilford once he knew their cousin had fully recovered.

Emily could not imagine the reason for tonight's gathering. Just last week, they had all been feted by the Prince Regent at Carlton House. He had offered a toast to the Beresfords as the kingdom's "National Treasure."

Emily had hoped she and Richard would be invited to His Royal Highness's Royal Pavilion at Brighton, as had Harriett and Lord Rockingham after they had thwarted a threat on the Regent's life, but Richard's investigation had not directly affected the Regent, as had the Rockinghams', so no such invitation had been forthcoming.

When the sweetmeats were laid, Devere stood at the head of the table, his gaze circling those seated around him and stopping at Richard. "First, I want to express my deep appreciation to the newest member of the Beresford family, even if it's just by marriage." His smiling eyes locked with Richard's. "It's my belief, which I believe is shared by my kinsmen who are seated at this table tonight, that my dear cousin Emily could have looked over the entire kingdom and never found a finer man than the Duke of Bentley." Devere looked to his immediate right, where Emily sat.

"Not the entire kingdom, my dear cousin, the entire world," she said with a smile.

Those around the table laughed.

Devere directed his attention at Richard again. "We are happy to have you in the Beresford family, Bentley, and all of us owe you a debt of gratitude."

"Thank you, my lord," Richard said. "I am the fortunate one to have married a Beresford." Her husband's loving gaze went to her, and she found herself sending him an air kiss.

"Next," Devere said, looking at his wife at the opposite end of the table, "my beautiful wife and I have an announcement to make."

All eyes went to Caroline Devere, who truly was beautiful. Emily thought there was just as much love in Devere's eyes when he looked at his wife as had been in Richard's when he'd looked at her. How blessed both women were. Indeed, both couples.

Caro smiled at the husband she adored. What a loving wife she had been throughout her husband's ordeal, never leaving his side.

"Just before I was injured," Devere went on, "we learned that my dear wife is breeding."

Exclamations rose from around the table. When the congratulations finally died down, Devere continued. "The surgeon tells us it's a miracle our babe made it through all the despair."

"I think he will be his father's son. A fighter," Caro said with pride, her shimmering gaze meeting her husband's.

Devere sighed. "I am the happiest man in the kingdom tonight. How blessed I am to have such a wonderful family and remarkable, beloved wife. And whether our babe is a son or daughter does not matter. Our child will be loved."

How Emily hoped she and Richard would have a son or daughter of their own. She was aware that Richard was looking at her. She looked up as he pointed to his chest and mouthed, "I am the luckiest man in the kingdom."

And she was undoubtedly the luckiest woman.

About the Author

Since her first book was published to acclaim in 1998, Cheryl Bolen has written more than three dozen Regency-set historical romances. Several of her books have won Best Historical awards, and she's a *New York Times* and *USA Today* bestseller as well as an Amazon All Star whose books have been translated into nine languages. She's also been penning articles about Regency England and giving workshops on the era for more than twenty years.

In previous lives, she was a journalist and an English teacher. She's married to a recently retired college professor, and they're the parents of two grown sons, both of whom she says are brilliant and handsome! All four Bolens (and their new daughter-in-law) love to travel to England, and Cheryl loves college football and basketball and adores reading letters and diaries penned by long-dead Englishwomen.

Check out these sites of hers:
subscribe to newsletter – littl.ink/newsletter
blog – blogl.ink/RegencyRamblings
website – www.CherylBolen.com
Pinterest – littl.ink/Pinterest

www.ingramcontent.com/pod-product-compliance
Lightning Source LLC
Chambersburg PA
CBHW070357200726
48294CB00003B/959

* 9 7 8 1 9 6 0 1 8 4 3 2 0 *